WASTELANDS

bandits, book two

BOOKS BY
LM PRESTON

PURGATORY REIGN SERIES

Purgatory Reign, Book 1
Deviant Storm, Book 2
Fierce Tides, Book 3
Colliding Souls

THE PACK SERIES

The Pack, Book 1
Retribution, Book 2

THE BANDITS SERIES

Bandits, Book 1
Wastelands, Book 2

LUV SERIES

Flutter of Luv
Thundering Luv
Double Trouble Luv

MIDDLE GRADE

Explorer X – Alpha
Explorer X - Beta

LM PRESTON

WASTELANDS

bandits, book two

Paperback: ISBN-13: 978-0-9841989-3-1

Edited by: Autumn Conley
Proof Reader: Dawn Yacovetta
Cover design by We've Got You Covered
Formatting by NovelNinjutsu.com

www.phenomenalonepress.com,
phenomenalonepress@yahoo.com

1

Daniel knew he must be psycho. With narrowed eyes, his fist tightened on his knife. He'd never change. Maybe changing just wasn't possible for someone who'd been raised a thief. His wrist flicked as he threw his knife into the dirt. Daniel couldn't deny the surge of energy that pumped through him at the thought of this new venture. He'd be lying to himself if he didn't admit that a part of him missed the heist jobs of his past – the brutality and challenge of it all.

"What do you think? Can we take 'em?" Gabe's deep voice taunted from behind.

Daniel couldn't help the smirk that slid in place. "Yeah. This job will be easy. We just might live through it if the Warden doesn't realize that someone like us would be crazy enough to break into this penal colony instead of breaking out of it." Daniel's eyes traveled upward to the yellow mooned sky, from the black terrain of wool-like grass shadowed by gold, and thought it deceiving for the atrocities he knew thrived on this dead planet. The place even smelled deceptive. The sweet perfume from scattered green and white flowers barely covered the metallic scent of fire and mildew in the air. He hoped the thick branches and overhanging dense leaves from the black barked trees around them would keep them hidden.

Gabe chuckled and slapped Daniel's back. "Only my boy Daniel would be insane enough to come up with that one. And me and my brothers, dumb enough to follow. Breakin' into a prison planet to save our kind, now that's a treasure worth saving, right?"

Daniel snorted. "Your brother Michael was the only one who wanted to come, but Franz wasn't interested, remember."

"I do, but a good fist to the face has a way of changing a person's mind." Gabe stepped up and suppressed his grin as Michael and Faulk handed them their guns.

Faulk's almond-shaped eyes narrowed as he frowned at Michael's dark scowl that matched his jet black whirlwind of curls, Michael's down-turned lips a signature look on his pale face.

Daniel adjusted his leather vest over his shirt, and straightened the belt that held his various weapons. "Faulk, why don't you, Gabe, and Michael scout out the quarter mile ahead?" His eyes traveled over the black and copper-ravaged lands of Uukin, the penal colony that captured and enslaved those of his kind: the Zukar, an ancient race of highly respected thieves trained to find and return coveted treasures throughout many worlds.

Faulk's slanted gaze pleaded with Daniel. "You know he doesn't like me. Spending time with the goon won't improve that."

Daniel released an irritated sigh, taking in his cousin's Asian features. "It's not about being friends, it's about doing the job."

Faulk frowned at Michael's back. "If he threatens me one more time, I'm done."

"I'll be the one threatening you if you don't get your head into this. Do the damn thing and just stop cryin' about it."

Faulk placed some chew-beef in his mouth, "I don't think landing here is one of your better ideas. Nickel is too young and inexperience to for a place like this."

"He'll be fine, like always," Daniel's eyebrow lifted at Faulk's shove.

"I don't think so," Faulk snorted, "but he wouldn't stay on the ship with Franz. I can't stand seeing a kid beg."

Daniel smiled at that. "Where else could we go? They've got every hiding place, peaceful planet and resting site flooded with security…and us on the hit list." His young brother Nickel had a way of manipulating them all. Especially him, since he'd been both mother and father to the kid since their dad got murdered. Being on the run from both criminals and Galactic police wasn't what he'd wanted for his brother, but it was the only life he could offer now.

"That may be, but you and I don't have to let Gabe and his brothers control this game. We're in it too. They didn't have to go on the run with us."

Daniel frowned at that. "Yes. Yes, they did. No way their father was letting Jade go with us alone – not after what happened the last time. And there was no way I was leaving without her. So we bring her brothers, and even though you hate Gabe, he's a good friend to me."

"Yeah, right. For his own purposes too." Faulk spat on the ground. "After this, we need to move on without them. I know a place where my father could make sure we have the protection we need from our enemies."

"I want nothing from your father. Him and my dad never saw eye to eye. After what we've done, your father's reputation as a Galactic politician would be in jeopardy if he helped me."

"You never know, he may have changed," Faulk added.

Daniel snorted, "Did you forget that I'm a convicted galactic felon?"

Faulk jerked his fingers through his straight black hair in frustration. "Sorry I brought it up – again. You know you're my blood. My family. I've got you in this, I just hope we don't hurt Nickel or Jade with this side trip to safety. Remember that place? You said you were leaving the life of gangs and crime behind you. I'm just wondering if you changed your mind. If so, pass me the memo, and I'll toss out my hopes for finding me my own girl, relaxing a bit, before I have to grow up and figure out where the rest of this life we are building as a family will lead."

"I got the message Faulk. Loud and clear. I need to pick a side, good or bad – but I'm not there yet. Let me stay in the gray and settle this. If we don't sniff out the source of this mess my father's death caused us – we can never have the life he wanted for me."

"Fine. We do this, then you figure it out. Not for just Nickel and me, but for yourself."

Daniel wanted the conversation over. "Stop stalling – catch up with Michael and do your job." Daniel held back a grimace

With a glare, Faulk stalked off towards Michael who appeared to ignore him.

Daniel mumbled, "If you didn't steal his stupid box to tick him off, Michael wouldn't be such an as—" He flinched when Jade bumped into him from behind.

Rapid footsteps pattered up behind Daniel, he braced himself knowing what was coming. Nickel sprang onto his back, and Daniel caught him, then flipped him over in front of him to set Nickel down.

Nickel giggled and punched at his brother's middle. "You're not supposed to catch me. I'm not a baby, you know. I can take you." Nickel slapped at Daniel's open hand.

"One day kid, but not today. I thought I told you to stay on the ship."

"Franz said he didn't need me there. I'd just get in the way and Faulk said he would come with me while I go on lookout. You know how green he is about these types of jobs."

Daniel sighed wanting to make sure Nickel knew their life of crime was behind them. "We're not training him to steal. We are here to get information, that's it. And maybe help some kids like us who ended up here for the wrong reasons."

"I know, but it's the same protocol right?" Nickel deepened, imitating Daniel's serious expression.

"Not exactly. All that stuff dad taught us — use it to survive, not take." Daniel picked a rock and handed it to Nickel knowing the kid collected them for his slingshot practice.

Nickel pursed his lips. "I know that. Remember I tried to tell you Dad wanted to change his life. Well, we're doing this, right? We just have to teach Faulk how to survive, I think his dad spoiled him, and that school he went to was stupid."

Daniel laughed. "Me too. Now go on and help our dufus cousin. Teach him the Zukar way, okay?"

"You can count on it!" Nickel ran off.

"Damn!" Daniel had fallen for it again, but he couldn't help it, he'd rather have the kid with him than on the ship.

"I thought you were going to watch your swearing?" Jade's soft voice teased. She tugged his dirty blond hair, which hung just below his collarbone.

Daniel's face broke into a grin as he pulled her into his arms and buried his lightly tanned hand into her dark curls. She let out a small sigh when he kissed her.

She pulled away reluctantly. "Franz is staying on the ship to watch from above. He has the force fields intercepted so we should go undetected for awhile."

Daniel's gaze flickered over in time to see his young brother catch up with the others. "Good, Franz's always been good at keeping us alive as our watchdog and getaway man."

"Yeah, that's what he keeps telling me."

Daniel straightened the strap crossing her vest that held her poisoned darts and knives. "Are you ready for this?"

"Why wouldn't I be?" Her hand rested on her hip in challenge.

"Because you've never done this before. A break-in job that could kill us all." Daniel flexed his fingers.

"Don't look so worried. I survived our last life or death adventure, and I saved your butt. The good thing about this job is – no one is sending *you* on it. We decide what we want to do, and not the Sira Zukar. Now admit it. I saved your hide. Remember?" A dark eyebrow lifted with a dare as she huffed at him.

Daniel let his pale finger caress her cocoa skin before dropping it to his side. He loved her new independence too much to remind Jade that he saved her instead. Many, many times, but he wasn't counting. He'd do it again and again.

"Maybe a few times. But if we're counting…" Daniel's gaze caught Faulk's signal. "Time to go." Daniel leaned forward and kissed her startled lips. Then stepped around her and followed the others into to the dark, dirt-covered terrain under the cover of the large hanging of dense dark leaves.

The itch in the back of his neck warned him something was out there…just before they were ambushed.

2

Feral creatures jumped up and out of the ground around them. Daniel shook off a momentary shock at their grotesque features. Lifting his knife fisted in his hand higher, his muscles clenched on the ready. Their flat tops, bulging lower bodies and multiple thin legs did nothing to soften their frightening image as they seemed to climb over each other in their haste for a meal. Mouths crowded with pointed teeth, chomped as the beasties surged closer. Daniel stabbed down into one of the attacking beings that had cleared the others. It reached just below his chest, making it easy to strike. His lips thinned, and euphoria bubbled up as he stabbed one, then another effortlessly.

"Yah!" Daniel screamed. At six feet tall, he was able to jab easily into their soft-spot just in the center of their flat form. The scuishing of their blood seeping out didn't deter Daniel as he kicked one, then another while his eyes darted around to find Nickel.

"Move it! I got to get to Nickel," Daniel roared, knowing that Nickel's short stature would make it easier for the creatures to eat him.

"I'll get him!" Jade raced past Daniel while she flung poisoned darts with such precision that the bug-like creatures dropped in her path.

"No Jade!" Daniel chased after her. He heard Michael's war cry, followed by Gabe's. His feet pumped faster. Branches hit, snagged, and pulled at him. Legs high, he broke through the black thicket of bushes just beyond where the attack began. Air drummed in his chest when his foot landed just past the bush. Squinting, against the gold moon's glow, which illuminated the hard curved tops of the creatures, Daniel headed towards the river of creatures attacking the others.

Daniel lunged forward slicing up the middle of one.

His lips turned down, "More! I'll kill you all," he spat. Its gurgling cry ended abruptly and it fell dead to the ground. He whipped around and shot one. Daniel slid his trigger fingered hand under his outstretched arm that waved his knife, while shooting one, then another.

Mucus filled blood littered the jagged path of deflated alien bodies ahead of him. He cracked his neck to the side, pushing down the tickling sensation of dread at not seeing Nickel anywhere in the chaos. Taking a moment to stand still, Daniel took a relieved breath at the waning numbers of attacking creatures and pivoted to catch up with his group.

Just as his foot reached the boulder, blocking the others, a beastie jumped on his back. Its strong legs braced behind him while its other thin legs held him in a vice grip.

"Ah!" Daniel struggled and squirmed, reaching for the spare knife on his leather belt. The thing's saliva dripped onto the shoulder of his protective black vest. Daniel's finger touched the hilt of his knife. A smile slid in place. Several teeth pierced his neck.

Blood drummed in his ear, "Ugh! Get the–hell–off–of me."

Daniel stabbed his knife between the multiple legs that held him. The creature jerked, pulling him with it to the ground as its legs loosened.

Daniel didn't hesitate. He twisted and sliced through dozens of legs before stabbing up into the thing's soft middle. Brown, puss-like, putrid-smelling blood soaked the ground while Daniel hopped up and back. Slipping slightly, he regained his balance. The others called Nickel and Faulk's names. The darkly dense trees muffled the sound. Daniel searched out more light. His chest felt heavy, but he kept listening intently for sounds that would lead him to the others.

Fear gripped him. *No God no, I can't lose them.* Daniel joined in the chorus of calls, "Nickel! Faulk!" and ran through the black, knee high bushes and trees scattered around him towards the others.

His eyes landed on Jade's stricken, tear-drenched face, and God help him, he was angry at her. At that moment – a part of him hated himself for being so careless. Daniel knew he was taking it out on Jade, but he didn't care. "What the hell have you done?"

"I-I. Nickel was just behind me." She shook her head and wrapped her arms around her middle. "Faulk was in back of him." Tears streamed down her face and she sniffled. "Then one of them grabbed at me and I dropped my darts. But when I turned…they were gone – both of them."

Daniel growled, his fist pumping in the air. "You stupid—ugh! I should never have trusted you do this." He growled. *"My family!* You let them take my freakin' family." He pointed at her. He was wrong so wrong, but he was too angry to care; it was too painful to accept that they'd been taken.

"Now wait a damn minute!" Gabe stepped up to him, his shorter shoulder hitting against Daniel's.

Michael silently watched from behind. His finger's caressed the hilt of his gun. "Give me a reason to set you straight. Just say one more word, and it's on."

Daniel took several deep breaths. He unclenched his fist, but his angry gaze never left Jade's stricken face. Remorse suddenly filled him. Daniel spun around, fell to his knees and pounded his fist into the ground. The cuts, the blood, didn't matter. He just wanted the pain to go away. Everything was going wrong. Seriously wrong.

"Daniel, I'm so sorry. So sorry, but the way…" Jade's voice cracked. "…the way you're looking at me, I think…it is best that we…" she whimpered.

He hopped up, took several deep breaths, refusing to let her ditch him first. Jade's insistence on ending their relationship renewed his unquenched anger. "It's over – we are over," he ground out. Daniel's gaze moved to Gabe. "Happy? It's what you all wanted, right? Well you got it." His hand gripped his gun and he walked past them. At that moment, his heart ripped, and his eyes watered, but he shuttered his lids against it. Not only did his heart feel as though it was broken, but he felt like a major creep. "Now let's go save my little brother and cousin." His head tipped to the side at Michael." You can watch her." Daniel couldn't get over Jade's reaction. He wanted to forgive her mistake – truth was he already had. But for her to throw away what they had so easily, it hurt. Deeply hurt. But now, it couldn't be helped. However, it didn't make it any easier to swallow.

Daniel made his way slowly through the brush. The others followed with the exception of Michael who was scouting out the land ahead. His mind wondered to the time he and Jade had spent on the ship to Uukin with her brothers and his family.

What have I done? His eyes slid closed against the painful throbbing of unreleased tears. *God, I love her.* Always had. Flashes of how Jade giggled when he'd hid and grabbed her to steal a kiss from the protective stance of her brothers. It was a major frustration for him.

The erratic emotions crowded Daniel, making him stagger in his haste. Their relationship was a constant argument between him and his best friend Gabe. It had fractured his and Gabe's friendship in some ways. Dating a girl he'd grown up with – one he'd treated like a little sister for most of his life, had serious challenges when her brothers didn't think he was good enough for her.

He'd failed Jade. Not to mention her father who sent his friend along to 'protect' her. More than likely to keep Daniel's hands and lips off of her. Up until they got off the ship, Jade's brothers had done a good job of keeping them virtually away from each other everyday. Daniel had even conspired with Faulk to divert her brothers on more than one occasion, which was probably the reason Gabe and the others didn't like Faulk much. They, more or less, tolerated Faulk since they considered him to be weak and never cut out to be a Zukar – trained thief.

He shifted at the sound of Michael's whistled signal that all was clear ahead. Gabe ran up ahead of him, barely throwing him a glance as Jade walked by.

Daniel's hand grabbed Jade's arm. She trembled and then become rigid. "Jade, I'm sorry baby," he whispered.

She nodded and removed her arm. "Me too Daniel," she swallowed. "Me too." She ran to Gabe.

Daniel's heart beat rapidly in his chest at the emotional blow she'd delivered. Remorse taunted him, but he didn't know how to fix the ridge he'd forced between them. However, saving his brother and Faulk pushed him forward into this failure of a mission.

Daniel approached the others who were clearing some of the thick brush so they could sit down. He stood in front of Michael. "What's the situation?"

Michael wiped his stained knife on his pants leg and tipped up his mouth to drink some vinixer that made it possible for them to breathe easier on Uukin for months at a time. He'd used some when they landed and it was time for a second and final dose. "Cleaners, the creatures are supposed to keep the border lands clear of runaways who made it past the two levels of guards."

Gabe stretched and took out some beef tack to chew on. "The buggers eat flesh but hate the bones. I suspect they take home food to their young, and that's where we have to go to get Nickel and Faulk."

Daniel plopped down beside Jade, who slid closer to Gabe. "Michael, you and Franz were studying this place before we came. Is there a short cut to get to them?" Jade's brother Franz was the oldest and the more experienced of their team. All were trained on the planet Merwin to become the best set of thieves in the universe. Daniel was honored and irritated that they'd left that life behind to follow him…to where? The prison planet Uukin. And for what? To join him on his bent path to change his life and live out his father's dream while getting his own personal revenge on those who planned to jail him on this planet.

Michael's eyebrow tilted. "Not one that many can travel at the same time. But I can attempt it." He stood and straightened his leather sleeves. "I'll meet you there, or the Row of Thorns, the first level of security."

"Michael, are you sure? Franz warned that if you go into their hive, you might not make it out." Jade's eyes filled with concern.

"I'll make it – with or without Franz's advice, but Nickel will be my priority." He nodded in Daniel's direction. "You got my word." Michael's rueful grin slivered into place, but it didn't reach his eyes.

Daniel studied Michael for a moment, not missing the fact that he didn't mention Faulk in his statement. "I need you to make Faulk your priority too," Daniel admitted to himself that he and Michael rarely agreed on much. However, Michael was a guy of his word. "Good, we'll meet up with you at the hive. We can make it to the hive in decent time." He nodded at Gabe, "May even beat you there." The old feeling of competition between them rose up to lighten his mood.

Gabe grinned. "I bet we will." He stood and pulled Jade up by the hand. "C'mon lil' sis, time for you to learn from the pros."

Daniel stood too. He surveyed the ground around them, then caught a flicker of light. Anxious dread hung in his chest when he recognized the gold trimmed handle peeking out of the soil. He bent and picked up Nickel's slingshot.

He stuffed it in his back pocket and tapped Gabe on the shoulder. "Let me talk to her a minute, 'kay?"

Gabe's jaw tightened. "Why should I—so you can break her heart again, like I knew you would?" He jabbed a finger in Daniel's chest. "I said you weren't right for her. I know you. Been your friend forever, and we are the same when it comes to girls. But you didn't listen, you just wanted what you wanted without giving her a chance to get someone better."

Daniel raked a hand through his hair, his eyes watching Jade's stiff back and Gabe. "It's not like that with her, and you know it. Just…just give me a chance to talk to her. I screwed up," his cleared his throat. "But I can't lose her okay? I…just…can't."

Gabe waved his hand up with a grunt. "Is this about the pakeet? That treasure those aliens put inside Jade, you and your family?" Gabe's forehead wrinkled. "You just want her for that, right? Only because you can't get the dumb thing to work if you don't have her with you."

"You are wrong. They took a part of me and put it in her because they knew I loved her like…like no one else. No one before or after her will ever get my heart like she's got it." He still regretted endangering her life to find revenge for his father's murder. It nearly got all of them killed. Yet, she fought with him, side by side, and loved him even as he pushed her away. Daniel had no words now. It seemed like loving her wasn't enough. To get her and keep her, he'd have to change for her.

Gabe snorted. "You gotta funny way of showing it, man." He let out an exasperated breath. "Fine. Take your shot, but you know she holds a grudge. And you crossed a line she never would've expected from you. I don't know why she's got it in her head that she should be a Zukar." Gabe smacked his palm to his fist. "Jade's not cut out to be a thief or a murderer – at least when it counts. Why you humored her in the first place I don't know. That's not the life my mother wanted for her. But I'll give you a shot – this time."

"I know, thanks Gabe." He didn't wait for Gabe's response but walked up behind Jade, barely touching her, it felt like every cell within him was alive and vibrating.

With her back towards him, Jade's hand came up as though she sensed his desire to touch her. "Don't even think about touching me, I know you don't want to anyway." Jade stood rigidly. "Daniel I'm sorry I didn't protect Nickel. I tried." She swallowed. "He was just out of sight for a second."

Daniel's hands dropped to his sides. "I get that. I was a cad and shouldn't have taken out my anger at myself on you." Hesitantly, he lightly rubbed the crease of her neck with his thumb.

She took that moment to turn around. Jade's gold eyes landed on him before she stepped backwards. Jade sighed and put some space between them. "You're mad at yourself? For what, Daniel? For trusting me…*go on and say it.*" Her voice cracked. "It was in your eyes when you looked at me." Jade's palm rested on her chest. "I felt it here, Daniel. The knife you stabbed through my heart when you wouldn't accept my apology." Jade's eyes watered, a look of longing conflicted with pain flickered in her gaze. "I'd be lying if I stood here and said I wouldn't forgive you for what you did – I have forgiven you." Her eyes dropped to her feet and she wiped away a stray tear, "And probably always will."

Daniel leaned in to touch his lips against her full ones. The zing of electricity that he'd always felt when kissing her made him feel alive. With shaking hands, she pushed him away.

"Babe, don't do this. Don't fight me, let me explain," Daniel begged gruffly.

Jade shook her head. "Explain what? That you don't trust my ability to be part of your Zukar team? And you think I'm a weak tagalong. The fact that you have me along because I'm your girlfriend. Well, I'm sure you won't have a problem finding another girl just like that," Jade snapped her fingers, "to take my place."

"No! There's no one else for me. You know I love you Jade." He kissed her hoping it was enough to prove how he felt about her. His heart jumped when she relaxed in his embrace.

Then Jade pushed hard against him. "Do you? I chased you first, remember?" Her hands went to her temples. "Just give me a chance to help save Nickel and Faulk, and we will figure out what to do about us afterward."

It took every piece of will he had to nod at her, before he said. "Anything – but this thing we have is not over. I – love – you with every breath I take. This is something I'm working on, can we just get past this. I trust you and your skills."

Jade crossed her arms, her eyes glassy with restrained tears. "Then try showing it. Your eyes don't say it…and earlier, when you were angry, you spoke the truth in your heart. What I've known all along – you want me to trust you, but you don't trust in me."

Gabe's deep voice broke into their conversation. "It's time to go if we plan on beating Michael."

Jade nodded. "I'm ready." Her eyes slid to Daniel before she turned away. She adjusted the belt slung over her shoulder that was full of poisonous darts.

"Me too, let's get them." Daniel gripped his gun and walked ahead of them. "I'll be the scout for the next mile."

Gabe spoke up. "Franz sent me a message that said it's about to get worse before it gets better. No help really. But he has us on the ship locator and is trying to lift some of the security barriers in our path. He said it gets harder for him to do the closer in we get."

"Tell me about it," Daniel replied and led them through the thick hip-high brush.

3

Michael was ticked. He'd had everything planned to precision, but Faulk mucked it up – again. Daniel must be blind to not notice how much he hated Faulk. Yeah, he disliked Daniel even the slacker's father, Rayne. But Faulk just rubbed him the wrong way. Having Faulk on this journey had done nothing but interfere with Michael's best laid plans. However, it couldn't be helped. Michael couldn't kill Faulk in his sleep like he'd dreamed of doing every night on the ship. Instead, he had to at least appear to tolerate the fool.

He cut through the brush, determined to beat Daniel and the others to the hive. Getting to Faulk before the others did was of utmost importance. The idiot stole something that Michael needed in order get what he'd come to this godforsaken hell-hole for. Michael didn't think the kid had it in him to actually steal something from him – but the bastard must've. He wouldn't underestimate Faulk again. Daniel's cousin would pay dearly for this irritation in his plan.

"Um…" Trees curved his path. Michael reached up at a hanging limb on the hair-covered tree. Its trunk was covered in copper hair-like moss and its limbs were thickly flanked in fat, black leaves that smelled like burning metal.

He spit on the ground as old nagging thoughts of Daniel urged him on further. Michael couldn't believe that his own father thought that Daniel held all the promise of a gifted Zukar thief. Michael always felt that Daniel was too soft, just like his father Rayne had become. The fact that Daniel's father was one of the best-known thieves in the universe didn't matter to Michael. Daniel didn't get the gift, and tarnished his father's legacy by turning away from the Zukar and setting out to 'change his life for the better'. Pitiful. Not only did Daniel endanger Jade's life, but had the audacity to think it was okay with Michael and his brothers that he could date her too. The thought of that slime ball touching his sister made him simmer with disgust. Daniel was weak and a womanizing pretty boy who had spent more time catching girls than doing his job for the Zukar. In no way was Daniel good enough for his sister. And his cousin Faulk was another joke. If Faulk hadn't stolen the key he'd kept hidden, maybe the wannabe Zukar would've lived through this job. If Michael didn't find that key, every reason he'd had for coming to this planet would be for nothing. One good thing he could say about Faulk was at least he didn't give up trying to be like a Zukar like his cousin Daniel did.

"I've got to get the gem back from Faulk, or his stupid ass will die. I swear." He growled, remembering his anger at Faulk's joke that sealed the newbie's impending death. The imbecile had attempted to prove he had the skills of a born Zukar, "Ha!" and stole the golden flat egg made of rare metal Michael had hidden. The egg was given to him for the sole purpose of getting him to the rumored treasure held by the Warden. It was in fact a key.

The small squattick climbed up onto one of the shrub tops where Michael was aiming his knife. Its small furry form reminded him of a porcupine from his father's homeland of Earth, but he didn't take time to ponder its purpose as he sliced downward on the bush, cutting the creature in half. The release of satisfaction rushed through his blood like refreshing water. Killing—now that was something he was born to do—and being a thief just gave him a reason to do it. The training he'd withstood in order to climb the ranks of the Zukar had been worth the praise he gained. He loved being one of the elite killing clean-up team youngest known members. He'd go in before the snatch team and silently dispose of whoever or whatever stood in the way of the job.

Michael reached the clearing that led to the inner circle of the wildlands. This area on Uukin wasn't under the Warden's tight control, but the land was dangerous all the same. Michael reached into the inner pocket of his vest and extracted a lit compass. Its face was flat, and the gold back rounded smoothly. He smiled at the heaviness of it. Rubbing his thumb over the silver face, he waited as the dial appeared like gathering sand on its surface, pointing south.

"Faulk, you better live long enough for me to yank that egg from your guts," he threatened as he moved slowly forward, testing the smooth rock surface leading to the edge of the wildlands. The ground was waved like cooled, brown, lava rock. He squeezed the handle of his gun just a bit harder and eyed the scattered boulders around.

Memories of what led him on this hunt drummed through is mind.

"Don't do this! He'll die," Michael screamed as the large men held his brother Franz while delivering another blow to his unconscious body.

The Sira Zukar's dark braid was pulled up on his otherwise bald head and littered with teeth from victims killed during snatch jobs he led in his youth. The man's sharpened incisors were filed into points to make him look more menacing. The shaved area circling the braid beaded with sweat as he pulled back his whip to deliver another strike to Michael's chest. "You will do this – kill Rayne's son for me, and recover the treasure, or I'll kill your brother right here."

"Screw you!" Michael spit at the Sira Zukar, but his bloody saliva hit the man's feet instead of his face where Michael had aimed. If he killed Daniel, his father would never forgive him. Neither would his brothers, and he wouldn't sacrifice his family for the two-faced leader of his clan.

"No, you're the one who's screwed. It will go in this order: Your soon to be dead brother first, and you — I'll enjoy your torture and death the most. Then your mother, and your father will be cut to pieces after unspeakable torture has been enacted upon them." He lifted an eyebrow. "Your choice, boy. You can save them all — just sacrifice Rayne's son. Then get the Fanyte knife filled with fire water from the Warden on Uukin. Or you and your brother are of no use to me."

Michael bit back against the vomit that rose up in his throat. He let out a groan as another strike from the whip hit the side of his face. Blood dripped from his wound and down his lips, and Michael couldn't control his broken response, whispering hoarsely, "I'll do it. You have my word."

Michael took a deep breath as another furry squattick dashed across the rocks. He lifted his gun and fired. The shot was silent, but the scream of the squattick as it fell with a twitch pierced the night. "I never liked you anyway, Daniel," he whispered.

Daniel's face appeared in his mind's eye to affirm his promise, the one pulled from his torn and ripped flesh to save his brother — his family, himself. He went to the creature and lifted it. Anger enveloped him like a cloak. He cut the creature through with his knife. He had to hold onto it since it fought feverously. His hate, his anger, his purpose, or the job wouldn't get done. "But in this I've got no choice. You'll die, Daniel. You-will-die." He popped a sliver of its flesh between his lips.

4

Daniel was angry at the way his life had played out. He was a cad. He didn't want to admit it, but the truth was best dealt cold. Taking it out on the task at hand wasn't even helping. He chopped through the briar-lands in hopes that the shortcut he directed they take would get them to Nickel and Faulk before Michael. One of the tall, sticky thorn-riddled vines pulled at his vest, but he chopped on, the pain a dull taunt from his troubled reflections.

Being the scout gave him time to think. Time to figure out how to deal with the bit of anger he had at Jade, at himself, his father and God for placing him in this life. Fessin' up wasn't easy to do. He was angry at himself because back at home on Merwin, he'd never made these mistakes. Back home, Nickel would not have come with him on missions for the Zukar. Those days are gone. Everywhere he went, he'd take his brother. His parents were gone, his uncle had disowned them and he'd never known his grandparents. Nickel was his responsibility. Ever since his dad got murdered for the treasure that threatened to destroy his home on the planet Merwin, he'd played the part of father and mother to his younger brother. And he sucked at it. Part of him still hurt just thinking about his home planet and what he'd given up to leave alive. Even though his father's body was no longer living, it was buried there. His mother's also. At least on Merwin, he could go see their gravesite, take Nickel to where their bodies rested so he'd never forget them. Daniel tried hard to keep Nickel connected to the memory of their parents and every time he did, it hurt all over again. He'd stayed up late with Nickel for hours past the kid's bedtime, relating stories of his mom's singing and his dad's boldness. If he were honest with himself, Daniel would admit to Nickel that the stories were for him too.

His father's legacy was on Merwin, the only home he ever knew, and a treasure trove of riches beyond reason that culminated three decades of his father's life. Gone to him now.

Daniel exhaled noisily. Frustrated that he was failing. If anything happened to his brother, he'd never forgive himself. But if Faulk got hurt, his uncle would go on a manhunt to find him. Nonetheless, it was the hand he was dealt. He just wouldn't – couldn't give in to it.

They had to stop. It was getting late and the snakes would be out if they broke through the briar-lands too soon. The creatures were in some type of dormant sleep unless disturbed when the thick pointed branches raked against their covered hideouts.

Michael probably could make it through the night if he went on the Eastern side to get to the hive. At least Daniel hoped so. He couldn't shake the thought that something in Michael wasn't clicking right. Something in their already-strained acquaintance had changed – but Daniel didn't know what.

"We have to stop." Gabe nudged him.

"I know. But let's get as far in as we can," Daniel answered.

Gabe twisted in front of Daniel. "I say no. If we go any further, they'll smell us. And I don't feel like killing no Snots tonight. It's too dangerous to do it in the dark, and using a light will only draw more out."

"Right." Daniel's straightened his back. He lifted his hand to brush a wayward blond curl from his face. But his eyes followed Jade who walked past Gabe to sit on the cleared ground. "I'll take first watch."

Gabe glanced at Jade. "She called it first."

"Well, I do it with her."

Gabe stayed Daniel's stride with a hand to Daniel's chest. "Look, don't push it. Give her a chance to get some action in saving your brother. You know…prove herself to you – to herself. Then it'll play out for you." Gabe blocked Daniel's view of Jade. "You really did it this time. I caught her crying because of the shit you did, and I'm working real hard not to knock some sense into my best friend."

"Stay out of it, Gabe." Daniel pushed past him, hitting his shoulder against Gabe to get by.

Daniel stood in front of Jade who rushed at wiping tears away. He tilted his chin up to the sky to allow her some privacy and asked, "Can you give me the mat for your brother to rest on?"

"Here," Jade croaked then handed him the flat mat that was no more than a few inches wide and long. It could be extended into a full sleeping mat, much more comfortable than sleeping on the bare ground. Jade sighed and turned away, pulling out a dart to rub through her fingers.

Daniel noticed the nervous gesture Jade used to calm herself in times when she was angry or sad. "Thanks, I'll take it to him." He just wanted to talk about something—anything that recalled the time when they didn't have these problems. Daniel squeezed the small, heavy piece of cloth on the mat she'd given him, unknowingly causing it to expand. By the time he reached Gabe, he had to toss the fully extended blanket that felt like it was filled with small grains of sand over his shoulder.

"Um, I see that didn't go too well." Gabe grabbed the mat from Daniel and started to flatten it on the ground with his foot.

"No, I just had to get my thoughts right." Daniel swallowed. "And she was uh…crying."

"That so? Well remember, just because she's cryin,' that doesn't mean she's not mad."

"I know." Daniel looked up at the gold moon then at Jade who was sitting on her backpack surrounded by curved up thorny vines since they covered most of the ground anyway.

"Man up, I'm going to sleep." Gabe lay down and turned away from him.

Daniel straightened his gait and strolled to Jade. "Move a bit. We both should be on watch."

Silently, she slid over to make room for him. Jade threw one of the rounded flat practice discs she used to throw darts at—about the size of the palm of her hand—on the ground in front of her. Her gaze was steady on the red disc while she poised her hand expertly to land three darts into its center.

"I bet you are imagining that is my face," Daniel joked.

The corner of her full lip hiked up. "Yep."

"Jade? Can we talk? Really talk about what's going on between us?" Daniel slid closer to her.

She sighed. "Do you think of Rayne often?" Her golden eyes studied him.

"My father? Yeah, a lot. Even… Nickel and stupid Faulk." Daniel bent his legs and rested his arms on his knees while rocking back.

"Tell me what you feel about Rayne now. Did you forgive him?" Her eyes studied Daniel intently, waiting for his response as if she was weighing some inner debate within her.

Daniel was quiet a moment. "I forgave him ever since we retrieved the treasure. When I found out he'd changed for me – for Nickel. I was stupid. I never should've been angry with him, but I thought I was justified."

"There's more, isn't there?"

"Maybe." Daniel didn't want to go there. To that place within him where he felt shame. Ashamed at the way he'd treated his father in the last days of his life. Even though at the time he thought he had a good reason to be angry, Daniel realized now that there was never a reason for his father to have to accept his disdain and disrespect for the years before his death. Did he forgive his father? Humph, more like he wished he could turn back time and beg for forgiveness. To be able to take back all the crude things he'd called his father to his face. To stop remembering the hate Daniel had held onto when he kept picking up more and more treasure hunting jobs with the Zukar, because his father decided to quit the business. Merwin had been a paradise, a deadly one that had left scars on Daniel he didn't know how to get rid of. But his father grew to realize that being known as a thief and a criminal wasn't the legacy to be left behind. Now he had to lay this to rest. It was too late to regain that security. Over. Done with. All Daniel had now was Jade's love.

Jade pulled out some dried squares of meat from her bag. She nudged him with her elbow to hand him one. "Just because we aren't together doesn't mean I want you to starve."

Daniel accepted the food, feeling the familiar flash of electricity her touch invoked. He wanted to kiss her, but instead licked his lips. "Thanks. What about you? Do you miss your parents?" Daniel chewed on the tough beefy tasting square before popping it into his mouth.

"Switching the subject's not going to stop me from asking the question again." Jade grinned at him. "Yes, I miss them so much. My mom especially. I never got to tell her how sorry I was or how much…I love her."

Daniel felt a twinge in his chest. His thoughts of his father were guilt ridden and filled with bitterness at his stupidity. He knew how she felt and sympathized with her. "I'm sorry about that. It's my fault for taking you with me." Daniel rubbed his hands on his pants. "You two never really got along."

"I manipulated you into taking me, Daniel. No way you were running from your father's killers without me." Jade pulled out more darts and absently tossed them with her chin tilted up to the sky. "As far as my mom and me getting along, we did, I guess, just in our own way. She wanted me to be the 'princess' of the family like she was, growing up. Mom was all dainty and feminine, I was skinny, and flat-chested with a big butt."

"Also, an annoying spoiled brat that I loved even when she was prankin' her brothers and me."

"The only reason I bugged you guys was because I got tired of being left out." Jade shrugged. "It got their attention," she looked at him ruefully, "and your attention."

Daniel tentatively touched the palm of her empty hand with his finger. "Jade, you know I'm sorry about what happened today, right? I really mean it. I didn't intend to lose my temper and be an ass."

"I know," Jade moved her hand from under his, "but I was hoping things would change between us – at least with this."

"It's hard for me – I want to protect you, keep you and those I care about safe. Why can't you let me do that for you?" Daniel put his finger under her chin to put her gaze on him. "Why do you fight your brothers and me in this?"

Jade pulled back from him. "Because I thought you knew me, Daniel. I would never cause Nickel to get hurt. Remember what we went through to save him before we got here? The way the Zukar turned against us and wanted you and Nickel dead. I fought that with you. I'd die saving him because I know how much he means to you — how much he means to me." Tears fell from her eyes. "And for you not to trust me to take care of him — for you to look at me with hate in your eyes," she shook her head, "you broke my heart, Daniel. And I don't think...I don't think it will ever be the same between us."

"It can if we keep trying. Just like we..."

Jade's hand came up to his mouth. "What if you, Daniel, were the cause of him getting captured? You could've been unable to save him. Then what?" Her hand dropped. "No more words about us. If we are going to try this friend thing, let's not go there, okay?"

Daniel couldn't resist kissing the palm of her hand; his eyes never left hers before she snatched it away. "Fine, but I'm warning you, Jade, I'm not giving you up." Daniel leaned back on his hands. "As for my dad, when I think of him, I feel like shit. I had it all wrong. I thought he'd given up on what he'd built as a master thief with the Zukar. Before he started refusing to do snatch jobs, I wanted to be just like him — a master thief. Hell, if I was honest, I wanted to be better than him. And for a while — I thought I was."

"Tell me about it," she snorted.

Daniel winked at her. "Don't help me beat myself up here, okay." He took a deep breath. "Remember that year I spent working those extra jobs for the Zukar?"

"Oh yeah, I saw you less — I sorta missed you." She crossed her legs and took off her vest to drop her collected darts in the protected pockets. Then draped it over her lap and started to clean off her darts.

"Believe it or not, I missed you a little too." His eyes traveled over Jade's full breasts, her dark hued skin and her black curly hair. He wanted to run his hands through it, pull her towards him and kiss her deep, like he used to do. But he knew that would be pushing her. Jade wasn't ready to completely forgive him. It showed in her tense shoulders and wary eyes.

"No way. You were too busy with your trail of girlfriends. I counted every one of them and would drill Gabe on who you were dating and when."

"That so?" He frowned. Daniel never considered those other girls as serious relationships. They'd been something to pass the time and he enjoyed them, every one of them in some way or another. But none of them touched him deeply like Jade. It was as if his heart was waiting for her. For Jade to grow up and become his. Daniel never told her that, but he thought he'd shown her.

"Yeah, but then you brought your silly cousin Faulk over, and I got distracted for a while." She smiled and got this goofy expression she always got when she was around Faulk. Faulk had made it his mission in life to make her laugh.

Daniel attempted to stifle that bit of jealousy he hid regarding Faulk and Jade's friendship. "Faulk was a prick, especially throwing in my face how hot he thought you were. And let's not forget that he considered himself the man for you when he first met you when we came to your house for your brother. The perv."

Jade rolled her eyes, "He's about your age right? Two years older than me? He's not a perv." Jade put the clean darts in her sack then took out her various knives to clean. "Well, he was the only guy besides you who got close enough for me to kiss. At least one my brothers didn't beat up or threaten to leave me alone."

"No worries on that – I beat his butt for good measure when he punched me for kissing you." Daniel lifted an eyebrow at that last statement. "Faulk kissed you? I'll kill…"

"No he didn't, but he wanted to. But after he knew I wanted you, he backed off." Jade blew at her curly bangs and tossed a knife into her open bag. "Stop switching the subject. Now, back to your dad."

"You got me." Daniel reached over and put a wayward curl behind her ear. "My father—God I hate thinking about this—he was unbelievable. Every job he went on, he was relentless…careful. I just was angry because he got careless and was killed because of it. Haden was weak, and under any other circumstances, my father could've killed him. But I had the feeling he didn't even fight with half his ability because he wanted to believe Haden was his friend. That's the only way I can see Haden getting the best of him."

"Why do you think he got careless? He was murdered."

"My father could kill any creature with his bare hands, and especially with a gun. But he didn't even look like he put up much of a fight."

Jade stuffed her vest in her bag. "Maybe Haden caught him by surprise – I mean, he was Rayne's best friend. At least his next best friend besides my father."

"Could be, but I wanted him to fight more, be more of the man I thought he was – knew him to be when I was Nickel's age. But when he refused to turn over his latest stolen treasure to the Zukar, I just didn't understand why. Then he was killed, and we followed his footsteps to get the pakeet. Until we all had a piece of the pakeet put in us and were able to bring Merwin back to life, I was too stupid to realize why my father changed."

Pulling out binoculars that were only a quarter inch in diameter, Jade unraveled the flexible rubber handles and placed them behind her ears to hold them in place. "That was when you learned he wanted you to be something besides a hitman. He wanted you and Nickel to do the right thing, to save people instead of hurting him."

"Right, Jade, now I hate that I can't see him. That I can't thank him for changing his life – for us, for me."

Crack. Snap. Daniel put out a hand on her arm to shush her. His fingers gripped his gun and he stood. He didn't bother to look back, but pivoted around at the ready.

Something scurried over his feet.

Jade gasped before jumping to action and tossing a dart downward. "They're coming out of the briar vines!"

The transparent creatures shaped like baby lizards with their bones, teeth and organs illuminated within their glowing, thin frames, rushed out of the thick briar vines. Pink tongues slithered out of their mouths. Their tongues widened like the noses of an elephant to suck at the ground. But their beady eyes studied Jade and the others closely.

Gabe yelled from a distance. "Don't kill them! They'll attack."

Daniel growled. "Then what the hell do we do? They're surrounding us." Swallowing his frustration, he breathed in, forcing his heart to settle.

Jade stood next to him, a dart fisted in her hand. "I already killed a few…is that why more of them are around us and not Gabe?"

"I don't know. Just stand still." Daniel exhaled in relief, now that the creatures seemed to stand almost frozen in waiting.

"They're not moving. You think they are going to attack?"

Daniel's eyes shuttered closed. "Just…be quiet, and still. They seem to be checking us out. If one of them takes a step toward us, then grab your stuff and run."

"Jade!" Gabe called. "Daniel…I'm stuck here like a statue. I sent Franz a distress call and he ain't answered. But I know the things don't do caves."

"What do they eat?" Daniel asked.

"Don't know…don't wanna find out."

5

An uneasy breath escaped Daniel's lips. "We can't stand here anymore. The briars will grow over us." He felt one of the glowing transparent reptilian looking creatures staring up at him.

Gabe snorted. "Tell me something I don't know."

"One's creeping closer to me," Jade hissed.

Daniel's finger tapped his gun at his waist, then traced up the leather strap from his pack that crossed his chest. "No choice in this, we gotta run for it. Gabe, what's up with Franz and the com?"

"Just got a chopped up map that appears as if he drew it himself and sent to me." Gabe snorted. "A line with an arrow then what I think…man, Franz can't draw worth snot. But it looks like some type of cave or something. I think we can stay there the rest of the night."

Jade spoke up. Her eyes blinking back her fear. "How are we going to make it out of the briars without being cut open by the thorns?" She gulped. "Just asking."

"Hack our way out." Daniel reached behind him, grabbed the hilt of his father's sword—the one left on the ship his father was gifted with by the alien race who'd changed his life—and his eyes slipped closed for a second with a slant slipping to his lip. Sweat beaded on his forehead, and his gaze collided with Jade's. "When I yell, stay close behind me. Don't – slow – down." He nodded at Gabe, who grinned. "Now!"

Without a glance down at the transparent beasties, he jetted into a run. Powerful strokes with the laser-laced sword cut through the briars like candy. He jumped over scattered patches, his arm aching and his cohorts' footsteps drumming behind him. Briars sliced at his arms, his vest, his pants, but didn't pierce his skin due to the protective leather-like material of his Zukar-made gear. And if Jade stayed close, she'd be safe from the thorns. That's all that mattered to him now, that she would be safe. They were almost clear.

"Gabe!" Jade's frantic call slowed Daniel's lead.

Daniel frowned with a growl. He whipped around and grabbed Jade by the arm as she'd stopped to pursue Gabe who was fighting off the transparent lizards. "He'll be fine. C'mon!"

She struggled against him. "I have to."

Daniel scooped her up and flung her over his shoulder. Not looking back, he continued his escape while tightening his arm around a struggling Jade's hip. "Stop fighting me so I can get us to safety!"

"You stupid meat-head! Put me down." She pounded his back with her tiny fist. "My brother needs us."

"Gabe purposely gave us that diversion! Let's use it." Daniel jumped over the last briar and landed on the smooth copper rock of the Windlands. His chest heaving, he slid Jade down to the ground and smiled back at her glare.

Her shoulders straightened, and she leveled him with an angry gaze. "Stop it. Just stop doing that. You could have told me he was diverting them so we could get away." Jade's hand waved in the air. "But no, you had to go all macho on me – like always."

Daniel sighed. "Why do you always have to take it there? Can't you just let me do what I've been trained to do? Take action instead of thinking about whether I'm hurting your feelings when I'm just doing what I gotta do to save our butts?"

Gabe broke through the dry briar branches, a dead beastie dragging on his foot and a confident smile on his scratched-up face. "What the hell took you so long to get out of there? I had to fight those stupid things off for five minutes."

Daniel threw a nod in Jade's direction.

"Me. I was trying to go back and save you." Jade blinked as though fighting tears. "But…I wrecked it up, again." She pivoted around and started to walk ahead of them.

Gabe slapped Daniel on the back. "Don't worry about her. Girls. No matter how hard a guy tries, he just can't make them happy."

Daniel shrugged. "Guess not. Change of plans. Let's get to the cave. We can't stay long, Nickel and Faulk might not last another day."

They headed quietly across the rocky terrain. Knowing they'd have to walk a few miles to get to the caves where Faulk and Nickel were most likely held. Daniel couldn't stop his jaw from clenching. He was just too damn mad, sad, and aggravated. Nickel and Faulk were alive – they had to be. Anxious energy rushed through him eating him up. He'd be lying if he tried to play off that after all that's happened in the last few months, he was back on his game. He wasn't. The night his father died in his arms kept replaying over and over again. The turmoil from his misplaced anger at his father at the time, hung on him like a cloak of lead. He couldn't shake it. Daniel had to find a way to deal with this or he'd cause them all to get killed. A heaviness Daniel knew would never go away.

His eyes roamed over Jade's petite, and slightly muscled figure. Her full hips and chest, framed by a riot of dark curls that spilled just below her waist made his chest squeeze. He'd ruined things with them, badly. Truth was Daniel couldn't help wanting to protect her. Jade had tried to train with them on the ship, but she just didn't have the edge it took to be a Zukar. Most women didn't even do field theft jobs. It was too dangerous and hard on the body – hell, on the soul. It changed you. Only thing was, that was all he'd been before his father's death. A wannabe killer and a great thief. It didn't serve him well. Now he was living in his own personal hell, all because he didn't see things clearly when it stood in the way of something he'd wanted. This thing with Jade was no different. He had to kick his habit of spitting out blame, it only ever pointed back at him – tenfold.

The waved rock of copper was teased gold by the glow of the moon. Daniel would have to sleep soon. Jade would have to also. But he knew sleeping next to her like he'd wanted to do for the last month wouldn't be possible now. On the ship, when they'd left his homeland of Merwin, he'd had to sneak kisses and time alone with her. Once he'd even managed to sneak her into his room where he held her in his arms dreaming she'd be his forever. After that one time, when Gabe walked in and found Jade in his arms, things had changed between him and his best friend. Now, Gabe and his brothers just wouldn't cut him a break and trust him alone with her. Willing to take his chances and push her just a little, he surged forward to catch up.

Jade walked stiffly ahead, not bothering to glance back.

Daniel came up alongside her. "Hey, you okay?"

She slid a dart between her fingers, a gesture that showed her anxiousness. "I guess so."

"Look, about what happened back there, I forget sometimes to clue you in on the way Gabe and I work together. We've been at this since we were little kids and can just read what the other one would do before it's done."

"It's alright. I understand how I'm not part of the club." Her eyes seemed to search the terrain for something.

Daniel's followed her gaze. Then he stopped mid-step. "That's Faulk's knife."

Jade didn't wait for him to head toward it before she jogged over and picked it up by the silver tipped bottom. The blade pointed down and was riddled with a gooey green substance. "Do you think it's a bad thing that the knife is here and not with Faulk?"

"Truth? I don't know what's worse, Faulk with a knife or Faulk without one. Sometimes I wonder what they taught that fool in flight school. Good thing is, though, there's none of his blood on the thing. So I hope that means they are still alive." He took the knife from her. Daniel would never forget the day he'd seen Faulk knocking at his door in Merwin as a flight cadet school dropout. He'd let him into the house and hid him there just to spite his father who hadn't spoken to Faulk's dad for over ten years.

Gabe came over to them. "A clue?" He studied the knife by leaning in. His blue eyes narrowed, while he flung back his dirty blond dreaded braids. "If they haven't eaten them by now, maybe they are saving them for their queen and we've still got a chance. From the last message Franz sent, the queen only comes out every few days to feed. He said the things were called Chickmu."

"Who cares about their damn name? I want to kill a few and save my brother and Faulk." Daniel wiped off the knife with a rag from his bag, then wrapped it up and put it in his pack.

"I got that, just trying to educate," Gabe's eyes winked at Jade.

"Let's go find this cave and get some sleep. We have to be on the move as soon as day hits." His heart raced up a beat or two with the hope that Faulk and Nickel were alive. And if he was betting on it, Nickel would find a way out of there. Maybe before they even arrived.

6

Faulk grunted. The black wood tree he and Nickel were tied to scratched his back. He looked over at Nickel and frowned at the knowing grin his young cousin gave him. "What you looking at? I'm trying to save us here."

"Okay, but didn't you listen to Daniel when he told you how to hold your hands when someone's trying to tie them?" Nickel looked at him, obviously trying not to smile.

"Maybe I didn't pay attention to that particular lesson, my little cousin, but I did listen when he taught me how to break out if someone ties your hands." Faulk blew at his bangs of straight black hair. "This isn't working," he said with disgust.

Nickel giggled and swayed his head from side to side. His spiked brown hair brushed against the black trunk at the tilt of his chin. "Daniel's right. That school didn't teach you nothin'. But don't worry, one of the guys will save us."

Faulk bit his lip and started struggling again. "Where's my knife?"

"Dropped it. Or was it snatched from you by one of the beasties? I don't remember. It's a blur." Nickel wiggled his shoulders trying to get comfortable. "If Daniel was here, he woulda broken a finger to get out of the ropes."

"Well, he's not here. All you got is me. And I'll get…us…out," Faulk said with another exasperated tug upward. "Screw it. I need to rest."

Faulk breathed in deeply. Searching out at the images around him for the others, the black rocks littered around him gave him a small bit of comfort. Just a bit. But it did nothing for the frustration he felt at himself. Leave it to him to get captured. And with Nickel no less. If it was just him, by himself, he would've been able to fight off the creatures. Ugh, who was he kidding, he needed Nickel a lot more than the kid needed him.

"You think they'll be back soon?" Nickel asked with a sliver of fear in his voice.

"I don't know. We researched this planet before we got here, but if I remember right, these things don't eat meat. But their queen does."

"Gee thanks, that's good to know." Nickel rolled his eyes, "It makes me feel a whole lot better."

"For an eleven-year-old, you got jokes?" Faulk snorted. "So, uh, I think they went into the caves." Above, the huge mountainous rock was littered with holed entrances to caves just big enough for the creatures to squeeze into. It made him wonder what the queen looked like. Faulk shook his head, admitting that he really didn't want to know.

"Do you think you'll ever want to go home to Earth?" Nickel's eyes blinked, and he sniffed. "I miss my dad so bad, sometimes, I cry about it."

Faulk adjusted his back and rested in a squat against the wood. "Sometimes I miss my parents and my sisters, but things with Pops got sticky before my graduation from flight school." The secret pocket on his pants rubbed the egg-shaped trinket he'd stolen against his backside and made him wince, thinking of Michael. "Besides, I don't know if I trust Gabe and his brothers when it comes to what we promised each other when this all started. We made a pact to change our lives, but I don't think Michael or even Gabe is on board with that."

"Maybe not. But what about you and what you want? You have a dad and a mom. Why do you want to stay with Daniel and me instead of going home?"

"I don't know, maybe because you and Daniel need me more than they do?" At least that's what Faulk hoped. The life waiting for him at home on Earth was filled with days of boredom and mimicking his father who was trying to make him into a carbon copy. It wasn't his dream, not anymore.

Nickel raised an eyebrow. "You think we need you?"

Faulk grinned. "I know you do. Daniel just hasn't accepted it yet."

"Maybe we could um, go home with you. We could live a normal life and be diplomats like your dad."

He snorted. "Daniel would go crazy living with my dad. Even I did. Besides, I'm sure I was disowned just like your father when he left Earth to run away from the law."

Nickel sighed. "I guess so."

He heard one of the beasties squeal. Faulk stood up and resumed his struggling in that moment. "I'm going to get us out of here. Trust me okay?"

"I did and it got us caught, remember?" Nickel lifted an eyebrow.

"Well, if you're so smart, why didn't you do that thing Daniel taught me about how to hold your hands out so you can wiggle out of a rope?" Faulk winced when hearing his knuckle crack.

"Ah, because I had three beasties on me to your one. It was kinda hard to concentrate when one's slobbering on you and the other's slimy legs are choking you." Nickel leaned his head back on the pole. "So, what did they teach you at that school anyway?"

Faulk tugged against the bindings on his wrists. "Lot's of stuff. How to fly any ship made in the universe. How to protect myself in hostile environments." Faulk squinted at Nickel's audible snort. "Also, how to read coordinates and speak over forty different alien dialects."

"Wow. Well, did you drop out before they taught you all that?" Nickel adjusted himself by tucking one leg under the other.

"Real funny, I see you and your brother think the same about me. Well, at least Jade sympathizes with my struggle through school and parents who coddle me."

"Only because she feels sorry for you." Nickel smiled.

"So what? A guy will take whatever the pretty lady is willing to give. Besides your knucklehead of a brother should thank me for all the diversions I've given them to be alone together. It's hard getting her brothers to let her out of their sight."

A loud rumble and minor earthquake shook the rocks loose from above. With a glance upward, Faulk worked harder at his binds. "Trust me, I'll do whatever it takes to get us out of this."

7

aniel flexed his fingers and headed toward the large boulder ahead. Jade had bedded down and Gabe was sitting up for the watch.

"I'm not sleeping yet." Daniel loosened his straps on his pack and leaned against the rock next to Gabe. "How'd you sleep?"

"Like a damn baby." He took a swig of water out of his canteen. "Until you slipped up and got the beasties hyped."

"Always got to rag me about my mess-ups?" Daniel kicked him lightly with the side of his foot. "Let's talk about this job. You know, go over things." Daniel worked hard to get his mind off his fear for Nickel and Faulk. It didn't help much that just four months ago he'd thought they were dead and he had to literally walk through fire to save them. It was the only way to get the treasure, the pakeet that saved his world, Merwin. Although, it felt like it happened a lifetime ago, Daniel would never forget the feeling when he thought he'd lost his family and Jade.

Gabe chuckled and cut his eyes at Daniel. "Playin' it safe huh? Not wanting to bring up my sister and your big ego mistake with that one, huh?" His chin tilted in Jade's direction. "Fine. Have it your way." He stretched and crossed his hands behind his head.

Daniel ignored the comment about Jade. He was done talking about her with Gabe. "The Warden, remember, we have to get to the chamber he guards to release the prisoners."

"Yeah, and I got that covered. Franz was able to figure a way around the force field the Warden erected around the upper hemisphere of the planet." Gabe straightened his leg flat on the ground.

"How? Did he send you a new map?" Daniel didn't doubt Franz's skills. He was one of the best younger guys Daniel knew, who could pull off something this big, but there were always unforeseen mistakes. Ones they couldn't risk here on Uukin.

Gabe's eyebrow rose. "He's good, but not that good. I got guess-ta-mates. Nothing perfect, but at least they should help." He lifted his sleeve and tapped on the band around his forearm. His finger pressed the middle while he waited for it to read his fingerprint. "Here, I'm sending it to your tech-did. Read it yourself, and you'll see why I wasn't bragging about how great it was."

"Good. When we meet up with Nickel, Faulk and Michael we can plan our attack on the inner fortress. No way they'll make getting in easy." Daniel hoped not. Having a diversion from the challenge, danger and pure adrenaline of a good fight always made him feel better. It was something his father had warned him could be addictive, and not always in a good way. Of course, that was the advice his father gave– after, he had decided to turn into a do-gooder instead of being the badass mercenary he'd been heralded for.

"Oh, we'll make it so," Gabe laughed. "It's easy enough since they've never in history had anyone break in. Remember, they take prisoners who don't have any family, that have been denounced from the Zukar and cast off of the planet Merwin for good."

"I know. Remember this is where the Zukar and the Merwin King wanted to send Nickel and me. But still, the Warden isn't a slack-off. He knows how to bring pain, how to dish it out, and how to maintain control. I don't expect this to be easy, but we *will* bring him down." Daniel wanted this. He wanted it because it could give him the best of both worlds. He could still do all the things he did as a Zukar, but he could do some good and free innocent people and realize his father's dying wish.

"Yeah, well, my father woulda stepped up and claimed you and Nickel. It didn't have to come to this. We didn't have to leave Merwin. If we hadn't, you would've become my real brother – at least by Merwin laws."

"True." Daniel pressed his Tech-did on his forearm. The 3D map of their route was broken in places and displayed itself in a muted outline on the ground. He touched the squared area that represented the prisoner fortress and it expanded into a map of the fortress that appeared to be both above and below ground. It sat on an underground river of fire water. "Damn. Firewater?"

"Humph, saw that, didn't you? That place must stink. Imagine being trapped underground and virtually set at a slow boil."

"But the Warden's body can withstand extremely warm temperatures. So can his guards. Unfortunately the prisoners can't." Daniel was sick at the possibility that was the fate that was waiting for him and his brother if they'd been imprisoned here? To be slowly roasted alive while the Warden worked them to death was why he wanted to see this place end. There were only a few dangerous criminals on this world. Everyone knew the only reason the Warden kept them here was to keep anyone from figuring out what he really did with the prisoners on this planet.

"Yep. Sucks for them. And us." Gabe smacked his teeth with his tongue.

"I'll figure out a way." Daniel waved a hand over the image. It appeared to collapse into the band on his arm.

"But can your cousin make it? Or will he wear us down? Put all of us in danger." Gabe's lips thinned and he cast a hard stare at Daniel.

"What the hell is that supposed to mean? He's my friggin' family. I ain't leaving him no more than I'd ask you to leave Michael." Daniel's muscles tightened.

"I know you and Michael never hit it off, but he's competent. We can trust him to do the job. Hell, I wouldn't be surprised if he got to them before us. He's a good Zukar – a natural thief. Even if he's a little brutal with his methods, Michael comes through every time. But Faulk is a joke."

"He's training. This is new to him and I'm working with him. He's not a thief – neither am I. Remember I left that life behind." Daniel rolled his shoulders as he balled his fist. He was sick and tired of Gabe's subtle hints on his disdain for Daniel's choice in changing his life around.

Gabe snorted. "How? It's a part of you. Just because you aren't 'stealing' for the Zukar, you're still a thief. You're 'stealing' the prisoners from the Warden. But if you want to sweeten the pot, fine. You can grab the Warden's prize possession: the legendary dagger of Fanyte – mystical fire water."

"I'm not stealing that. I'm freeing friggin' prisoners who were enslaved here because they didn't have anyone to defend them against Merwin's politics." Daniel jutted up. "Remember the promise you made to me when I told you I was leaving that life behind. That I was following the destiny my dead father wanted for me?" He pointed at Gabe. "You promised you would redirect your purpose in life too. And whether you want to or not, I don't give a damn, but don't drag me down that path again."

Gabe broke into a grin. "I meant what I said. But if given the chance at that treasure, before the Warden uses it on us, I'm taking it—and I advise you to take it too."

Wordlessly Daniel stared down at Gabe, who finally relented and looked away. Daniel gritted his teeth as Gabe lifted the canteen of water to his lips. He wiped a hand down his face and walked over to where Jade lay. He had to put some distance between him and Gabe before he lost his temper and punched him in that taunting grin.

He studied Jade's relaxed features, comforted that at least in sleep, she trusted him and Gabe to protect her. Giving into his desire to be close to her, he lay down next to her and pulled her into his arms. Daniel relaxed a little and let out a breath as Jade turned around in his arms, draped a leg over his hip and sighed contentedly.

Someone was kicking Daniel's leg. He mumbled, "What?"

"Let go of me." Jade's delicate hand smacked his face. "Stand. Gabe said we need to leave now."

Shaking his head, he dragged himself up. "I hear you." Daniel stood. He adjusted his pack, which was slim but firm at his back. Then leaned down and picked up his sword that was collapsed in its case. He slid it in the loop between his back and the pack.

Jade watched him quietly.

"Jade. We'll get them back." He nodded at her. Daniel hoped she believed him. He wanted her to see that he was remorseful. Maybe she did and just wasn't ready to forgive him. But after all they'd been through in the last year, she should know, time waits for no one, and tomorrow wasn't promised to them, at least with the way they were living.

A rueful smile tilted on her face. "I hope so. Because if we don't, I think our friendship will end. What friendship we do have will never survive me causing you to lose your family." She swiped a stray tear from the corner of her eye before turning away.

Daniel stepped to her. "Yes, it will. But don't doubt that your brothers and I are good at what we do. We'll get them, and take care of what we came to Uukin to do. The way I feel about you goes so much deeper than you know. I made a mistake. I have a temper. I lashed out at you and you didn't deserve it. Forgive me and let's work this out."

"Not yet. I can't." Jade's hand traveled down the strap on her chest that held her darts. "Daniel. Um…I will fight with all I have to save them. You know I will, right?" She nodded.

He smiled, genuine, knowing she truly believed it. "I know." He reached over to touch her cheek.

Jade pivoted away before the caress.

8

Michael was almost there. The tunnel he'd discovered on the map, given to him by the Sira Zukar, gave him the edge he needed to stay one step ahead of Daniel. It was cold and moist. Darkness engulfed him and the thin light, hooked off his ear, kept it at bay. The dank smell of water and dirt, mixed with the stench of putrid minerals, enveloped the tight space.

Even though Michael had been trained at least two years prior to Daniel, and had gone on more dangerous missions, Daniel's previous number of successes had been higher, at least by Zukar standards. Fortunately, Daniel hadn't gotten promoted to the cleansing team.

Michael had been on the cleansing team for almost two years. He'd been trained to kill disturbances to the treasure hunting missions quietly and effectively. His skills were endless and included the ability to dispose of numerous species throughout the universe. Michael's father had trained them since they were just toddlers.

Michael snorted as he recalled that none of his other brothers were selected to pursue that faction of the Zukar. He searched up ahead. Michael tilted the small flashlight on his ear and adjusted the glow to a larger size. A bit further down this tunneled path and he would be under the area where the Chickmu kept the queen's food.

He didn't plan on letting Faulk or Nickel survive. Once he got what he came here for, he could travel to the inner layer of the fortress faster without the extra baggage. Unfortunately, because of Daniel's stupid cousin's sense of loyalty, it would be best to finish him off. Otherwise, Daniel would know Michael's compliance was faked. Besides, that was the bargain he'd made with the Sira Zukar. His parents' life, or Daniel's. To Michael, there was no question what he valued more. He neglected telling his parents before they left Merwin since it would've been useless to convince them what had to be done. His father would've insisted on fighting the Sira Zukar face-to-face. Useless. It was stupid to even consider it, but his father seemed to be struck dumb when it came to his dead best friend, Rayne and his sons.

A moaning noise vibrated softly behind him. It was a good indication that the Danum creatures that created these tunnels were a distance off. Only the young ones moved fast enough to catch a victim unawares. So Michael took his time reaching in his pocket and pulling out a laser knife to cut through the dirt. He twisted the small, bendable flashlight at his ear, applied some pressure and was rewarded with an x-ray image of the world above.

Dirt rained down in front of him. He hopped back before he was drenched in the heaviness of it. A mound of gravel piled in front of him and the dim light from the sky cast a gold glow on the top of the hill he'd created. He brushed off his hands and climbed the mound of rock and debris. With a tug on the side of his belt, a hook extended and he pulled on it then tossed it up to clasp on the edge of the hole he'd created.

He flicked the release on his belt and held on while he was pulled up. His gun firm in one hand, Michael dug his other hand into the dirt as he climbed up and out of the hole. Wiping his hands on his pants, he looked around for any of the creatures. Michael took a deep breath since the air was a bit better than below.

Nothing. Good. He walked over to where the map indicated the creatures held their offerings for their queen. Nickel and Faulk were tied to wood poles in the middle of a clearing surrounded by mountainous rock riddled with holes he figured the creatures lived in. Faulk's head was hung to the side as he slept, but Nickel's eyes landed on him.

"Michael! Hurry." Nickel was jumping up and down as much as possible with his hands bound.

Faulk's head sprang up, a surprised yet sleep-dazed expression on his face. "Michael?" He recovered quickly and added, "Over here. What are you waiting for? Save us!"

Michael stood there. Just staring at them for a moment and crossed his arms. He tightened his jaw and walked over to Faulk. Smacked him awake, then lifted his head up by the hair. "You have something of mine. Give it to me if you want to get free."

The fake expression of innocence Faulk delivered disgusted him. "I've got nothing with me that you want. Just let us go. Get us out of here before they come back!"

"Making demands?" His eyebrow lifted. Michael planned to leave him right there. But he had to get what he'd come for to save him.

Nickel looked from one to the other, "What's wrong with you? Let-us-out!"

"You," Michael backhanded Nickel. "Shut up!"

Nickel was stunned to silence, then released a whimper.

"Now Faulk, if you don't want me to shoot you and your 'cuz, you will give me what you took from me on the ship." Michael's gun was pointed dead center at Faulk's chest.

Faulk shook his head. "I don't know what you're talking about." His face went through several expression, obviously struggling to keep a straight face. But the sweat wouldn't stop beading up on his forehead.

Michael knew his anger, even hate had never been this apparent before. "So you want me to beat it out of you?" he sneered. "I'm not Daniel, I won't hold back." He punched Faulk in the stomach, the chin, the chest over and over again. "Give it to me!"

Nickel screamed. "They're waking up!" He struggled and yelled when he pulled an arm free from his binds. Blood dripped down his hand from the scratches.

Faulk pleaded. "Michael help us – please!" His eyes skipped nervously toward the creatures pouring out of the holes in the caves around them. Their many snake-like legs crowded their bottom half as they ate up ground, closing in on the clearing. "You've got to help us first."

Michael stopped his pounding on Faulk's stomach and stepped back. His stare was unrelenting, yet he held his hands coolly to his sides.

Spitting a bloody wad onto the ground, Faulk bargained. "I slipped that gold piece I lifted from you into Daniel's things, I think," he stated. "If you help us get back, I promise I'll get it for you."

A growl escaped Michael's lips. "You better be telling me the truth. If not, you're dead and your cousin won't even be able to save you from me." He cut Faulk loose.

Nickel rushed behind Faulk to snatch the ropes away. Nickel did it so quickly Michael couldn't tell if Faulk appeared to be lying. And Michael didn't have the time to search him to prove it.

"I need a weapon," Faulk said.

Michael tossed him a knife. "You better be able to fight." He lifted his gun and shot one of the charging creatures in the eye. Another, and another fell from the rain of gunfire he sent in their direction. "Follow me to the way out."

"Ahhh!" Nickel screamed when one of the creatures jumped on him. Struggling, Nickel's fingers sank in one of the creature's eyes. Michael's bullet connected. The creature jerked backwards.

Michael ran towards the hole he'd climbed up, not caring whether the others were behind him or not. Anger at wasting time on Faulk's excuses kept him from making sure the guy was behind him. But there was no doubt he was, since he heard Nickel's feet pounding behind him, and stupid ass Faulk screaming.

His arms pumped, legs pushed across the rocky pavement. Dust flew up around his calves and his lips pressed together as he dropped down into the hole.

9

Daniel pounded the rocky ground with his boot. Black sprouts of wood poked out from the pebbly floor. He didn't look back at Jade or Gabe. He just pressed on. They didn't have far to go to get to the place where he believed Nickel and Faulk were. The firm set of his shoulders started to ache, but he didn't focus on it; he only studied the land in front of him, seeking out any clue.

The conversation with Gabe ticked him off. Gabe knew he was trying to put the life of a Zukar behind him. Hell, Daniel would be the first to admit that leaving behind everything that had made him into the guy he was today was crazy. When he had thoughts of the future, his mind drew a blank – unchartered and confused. If he was honest, part of himself teased him – reminded him that he couldn't ever change. Once a thief—a killer in training—always one.

In truth, he had no real idea of what the landscape of his future would be beyond saving them and getting off this planet. Coming here, hadn't been the best decision. It was the closest place to his home planet, and allowed him the opportunity to bury the demons of his past while doing something good for once. Something that involved saving others because it was the right thing to do, and it didn't payout the big amount of riches that all the previous missions he'd had with the Zukar did.

He slowed his pace and glanced back at Gabe who was talking to Jade. Daniel felt like Gabe had punched him in the chest by taunting him to steal the Fayte. Was Gabe with him on his journey to changing his life, or was Gabe just holding him back? Whatever it was, they were on this world together. All of them were dead to the Zukar now and Gabe as well as his brothers could never go back to Merwin without knowing they'd be hunted and tortured for their betrayal. If they continued to live as Zukar off of Merwin, without the protection Merwin provided, the Galaxtic Police would capture them and take them to some mind-altering rehabilitation program that they'd leave as walking zombie yes-men. So the only thing they could do was change, stay off Merwin, and hope Gabe's father would keep his promise to meet up with them on Earth.

"Daniel! Slow up," Gabe called.

Daniel stopped and waited. He didn't want to talk to Gabe, but it couldn't be helped. So he stood there with every muscle on his body clenched.

"What's the plan when we get there? We don't have far to go," Gabe said. "I have some explosives on me. We might need them."

"I know we'll need them, but I don't want to use them if we can help it. The noise and commotion might tip off the guards." Daniel wouldn't look at him, but just stared at the silhouette of rocks and mountains ahead of them. It wasn't until now, at this time, that he'd ever remembered being this angry at Gabe.

"You hearing me?" Gabe tapped Daniel's arm with his fist. "I'll take the lead from here."

Daniel nodded then went to stand next to Jade while Gabe walked ahead of them. "Hey."

"Hey back at you." Jade smoothly walked alongside him.

"Did you sleep good?"

"Sorta. I just can't stop repeating the scene of Nickel being taken. And Faulk fighting to get to him." Jade's step slowed for a moment, then she quickened her pace.

"That happens to me too. I keep trying to think of what I could've done different."

"Nothing." She swallowed. "Except maybe to stop me from going after them."

"Let's not talk like that, Jade. I told you I forgave you. That it's over. Can you just let it go?" Daniel reached out and tugged at her arm. His eyes stared at her lips. "I really just want to kiss you – I *need* to kiss you. Maybe it will take all this…stuff between us away."

Jade's eyes watered. "Maybe," she whispered.

Daniel's hand was trembling. Damn, he couldn't believe it. Since the moment she'd dared him to kiss her months ago, kissing her was as necessary as breathing. And now, for her to give in this one little gift, his mouth was watering for it. He slid his hand along the curve of her chin, and teased her ear with his finger.

Jade's breath caught in her throat, and she licked her lips. "Just kiss me before…I remind myself we're just friends."

Slowly he leaned in and whispered, "Friends kiss friends when they need it." His lips barely touched against Jade's. Daniel felt her shiver, and he teased her lower lip before pressing closer and delving inside just as she sighed his name. Flooding of electricity tickled the hairs on his arms and he felt starved for more. More of her, more of the warmth, forgetfulness and softness she gave him.

Jade's palms flattened on his chest, "Stop." She stepped away. "This is so confusing. Too confusing. I'm…" Tears welled up in her eyes. "I can't do this." She rushed off.

Daniel stood there with his arms still open, dazed at her sudden departure. "Damn."

They slowed their progress. The sun was low in the sky and they'd just cleared the two mountains leading to the creature's hideaway.

Daniel hiked up his gun. "It's too quiet."

Jade was next to him with several poisoned darts threaded through her fingers. "They've got to be here. It's where Franz said they'd be, and he should know."

"I know Franz knows, but if it's quiet—this quiet—it might mean," Daniel couldn't say it, wouldn't state what his heart wasn't willing to believe. He'd kill every one of these things if his brother and cousin were dead.

"Over here!" Gabe's insistent whisper and waving hand beckoned them.

Relief flooded Daniel's veins. "C'mon." He jogged around a large boulder to join Gabe who stood in front of two darkly charred wood sprouts from the rocky ground. Daniel walked around in a circle searching for clues that Faulk and Nickel had gotten away.

"They're not here," said Gabe.

"What?" Daniel frowned. He bent and picked up the scattered pieces of rope on the ground. Then he studied the surface closer and recognized scattered footprints—human ones—large and small. Daniel followed a few of the smudged prints, which were vaguely outlined with the dust that was scattered on the rock-covered land. "Michael was here."

Jade came over to him. "Do you think he took them with him? Or maybe they got away on their own."

"No. I don't think they did." Daniel tossed the rope down. "Michael cut one of the ropes. Probably Faulk's since Nickel would've been able to get out of his – eventually."

Gabe chimed in, "Then that's good. We could meet them."

"Can you contact him?" Daniel asked.

"Negative. Remember the force-field and we don't want too many coms to alert the guards that we are here. Besides, Michael hadn't checked in—not even with Franz." Gabe played with the mini-computer on his wrist. "And Frantz conceals his signals by sending them in time with the security beacons on the outer hemisphere of the planet."

Daniel tucked his gun back in his belt. "Good. Then there's one thing I want to do before we leave."

Gabe eyed him. "What?"

"Something to make me feel better." He spat on the ground. "Kill their queen."

Gabe grinned. "I like the way you think."

Jade rubbed a dart between her fingers. "Point the way, guys. I want some revenge too."

Daniel didn't savor the moment from Jade's happiness, even though he was the reason for it. He just pulled out his gun, strode in the direction of the queen's cave, and snatched out his climbing rope. The hook from the tool was heavy in his hand. When he came to the base of the mountainous cave, he pressed a button on the side of the hook.

It sprang out from his hand with rope trailing behind it and hooked itself on the inside of the cave above. Jade rushed forward. "Girls first."

Daniel slid to the side and held the rope while Jade climbed gracefully up to the mouth of the cave.

"You go up after her. I'll stay here and watch for more of them." Gabe grabbed the rope from Daniel and secured it for him.

Daniel worked harder at climbing. He didn't want Jade up there by herself any longer than necessary. Since any alien on Uukin could be unpredictable and deadly, he wanted to use some caution before killing the thing.

Jade reach down and helped pull him up and into the dark cave. It smelled of rotted flesh. Daniel supposed the queen would eat her subjects if there was nothing else available. He just wanted to kill the thing and make sure they wouldn't be her next meal. Not only that, but his father once told him to never leave his way out of a place unclean. And killing the queen would weaken these things if they had to come back this way after they freed the prisoners.

Daniel stood at the entrance of the cave with hand up, motioning for Jade not to move. Listening for sounds, he only heard a faint dripping.

His mouth watered. Blood pulsed through his heart. And he was loving it. The feeling of being Zukar—the one in control—fed him like a starving baby. Thankfully, Jade was quiet behind him.

"What now?" she whispered.

He put his finger up to his lips, slightly irritated at her naiveté. Truth was, he'd rather she stay with Gabe, but he knew she would bristle at the notion. And Daniel wanted to take one step towards making Jade happy, so he tamped down on the anxious feeling within him.

Daniel stepped forward and softly he let the tip touch the ground before putting down the full weight of his body on his foot. He heard Jade's tentative progress behind him. He reached for his knife knowing he'd have to make a quiet kill or they would be overrun by beasties coming to protect their queen. And that would mean a sure death for one if not all of them.

The cave was only a few feet taller than Daniel's six-foot frame, but was rather wide and the sides seemed to sweat moisture. He halted his stride to activate the night vision device hooked on his ear. The small rubber piece fit around the curve of the back of his ear. With a pass of his finger, a pulse of energy left the device and emitted a clear 3ft by 6ft image of the cave in front of them. It appeared as though he was looking into a clean window framed in darkness.

Daniel scanned the ceiling of the cave and noticed small flat eggs were stuck to the surface. A gooey green substance glued them to the wall of the cave. There were only a few near the mouth of the cave where he stood. Progressing forward, Daniel counted more and more. His heart raced in his chest. Up ahead of them, in the dim interior of the cave, there was a shadowed area littered with dark lines that protruded from a blob of a figure in the distance. Daniel halted.

Jade bumped into his backside. "That must be her. It looks like she's sleeping."

He nodded, and waved his hand at Jade to follow.

"I'm thinking we shouldn't do this," she whispered.

"We have to if we want to come back this way. Kill off a threat. The way we were taught."

Something moved in the belly of the cave, from their viewpoint, it was hard to make out. Daniel studied the area trying to gage what they were up against. He adjusted his device to zoom in. He stood perfectly still as red eyes met him with a hungry stare.

The queen was awake.

Daniel put out a hand to stay Jade's movement.

She peered over his shoulder and gasped.

The queen's body was a mass of tentacles that spewed from the top of her head and down the sides of her body. Two large appendages were spitting out a gooey liquid over a few eggs on the ceiling.

Every muscle in Daniel's limbs poised for attack. "She's coming."

At the vibrations of his voice, the queen let out a shriek and with several pops her tentacles disconnected from the walls of the cave. Moisture dripped repeatedly from the wall as if her tentacles had been draining the surface of all its fluid.

Daniel fired his gun at the queen's chest. Bullets bounced off her. The creature pounded her tentacles at the ground. His heart thudded in his chest, but he dug in and ate up the adrenaline pumping through him.

Jade screamed, releasing several darts that stuck out of the creature's eye.

"She's not easy to kill!" Daniel aimed toward her mouth, which was riddled with massive teeth. He pushed Jade back. "Get out of here!"

A roar came from the exit of the cave. Gunfire outside drummed through the cave.

Jade pulled at Daniel's shirt. "Gabe's in trouble!"

One of the queen's tentacle's grabbed Daniel by the neck, lifting him up into the air. Daniel twisted and pushed Jade off him. He reached for his knife.

"Daniel!" Jade threw a multitude of darts with precision. Some landed on the wrinkled skin of the queen's face, some in several tentacles and one on her tongue.

"Go dammit! Leave!" Daniel croaked. He had one arm around the queen's tentacle. Wrapping a leg around another, he hauled his body close to her mouth. "Ahhh!" He stabbed into the soft tissue of her tongue and sliced down her mouth.

The queen's hold faltered. Daniel relentlessly sliced through the leather-like muscle of her neck. Yellow blood seeped out and it dropped to the floor with Daniel falling upon it.

Jade's fingers grabbed at his shoulders and pulled him up. Daniel grabbed her hand and ran toward the sound of a battle.

"You should've left." Daniel yelled when they reached the mouth of the cave. His muscles were keyed up and his teeth clenched at the view below.

Masses of creatures were pouring towards Gabe from all sides.

Gabe screamed, "Get your asses down here! NOW!"

Jade hesitated, second-guessing the jump.

Daniel let out a grunt, not having time to think about her feelings. He wrapped an arm around her waist and leaped. The rope dangled in front of him. Forcing himself not to react to Jade's screaming, he grabbed the rope.

Held on for every inch of his life. It burned and his hand bled as he slid down the rough fibers. "Yahhhh!"

"Daniel! The rocks!" Jade screeched.

Daniel braced himself and spun his body around to protect Jade from the impact. "Ugh!" His back hit the jagged rock. Light formed behind his eyes and he shook it off. Jade's arms tightened around his neck and shoulders. But he never let go of the rope.

Gabe yelled, "I'm throwing bombs! Move it."

Taking a deep breath, Daniel mentally hyped himself into pulling at the last bit of strength in him. His face throbbed, his chest ached, but he shimmied down the rope. Jade jumped off his back to land at the small safe place behind Gabe. Daniel followed, fighting against wobbly legs and exhaustion.

Daniel swallowed back a curse. They were surrounded by hundreds of the creatures.

Gabe threw a smile over his shoulder at Daniel. "Ready?" He used a small tube device to spew fire in semi-circle around them. The creatures fell back a bit.

Daniel nodded. "You got an escape plan?"

"Yep, just run through the dead bodies. And follow me!" Gabe tossed several small silent bombs in front of them. The creatures were incinerated once the device hit the ground pushing its powerful pulse of power outwards. Instantaneously they were dematerialized in silence.

Daniel reached for Jade's hand. She fought against it briefly.

He was insistent. "Stop. I will keep you safe." He didn't spare Jade a glance when her hand relaxed. His eyes never left the mass of creatures that were kept at bay by the small fire line barrier Gabe had erected.

"Five, four, three – oh hell! Now!" Gabe flicked the detonator in his hand.

Daniel raised his gun. A smirk slipped on his face. His fingers squeezed Jade's. He vaulted into a run. Explosions sparked around them. Run. Pull. Dodge. Daniel held Jade's hand, ducking out of the way of a burnt flying tentacle. Gabe was ahead shooting, and blasting their way clear. The screeching from the dying creatures almost sounded harmonic in rhythm to Daniel's pounding feet.

Can't stop. Push harder. Daniel dragged Jade behind him. Then slid out of the way of a careening burning creature. Gabe jump down into a hole just beyond the stakes that had held Faulk and Nickel. Daniel couldn't stop the electrifying tingle flowing through him at beating the odds against the Queen, whose minions had stolen his brother for food.

"C'mon!" he yelled back at Jade.

"I am!" she responded and released his hand to run next to him.

They raced to the jagged hole in the ground. Jade's leg jutted out as she jumped. A snake-like tentacle grabbed her by the arm.

Daniel aimed his gun. "Die bastard!" The laser-shaped bullet sliced through the alien's arm.

Jade screamed and fell into the dark hole and Daniel lunged behind her.

"Got her!" Gabe grunted as he caught Jade's slight form. They were thrown backwards into the dirt floor of the Danum cave.

Daniel mentally loosened his muscles to brace for the face-forward fall. He pushed his hands out, concentrating on the ground, then connected and forced himself forward into a roll. Landing on his back, he winced. The pain was never something he liked about his training as a Zukar. He bared it, but his father had seemed to be immune to the aches and rips on his body when he was alive to teach Daniel how to mentally dull out the consequences of being a master thief. It didn't matter now; his father was gone—never coming back. And Daniel was here to hold what was left of his family together.

"Daniel, you okay, man?" Gabe grasped Daniel's wrist and pulled him up.

"Yeah, I'm alive." Daniel searched beyond Gabe for Jade. "Where's Jade?"

"I sent her ahead. It's safe. The Danum are in the back tunnels, I'm sure. But you looked like you dazed out there for a minute."

Daniel dusted the dirt off his smooth pants. His fingers mindlessly tugged his vest in place and straightened the bag on his back. "She okay?"

With a nod, Gabe slapped him on the shoulder. "You know it. I'm making sure my little sister's okay. I screwed up once—but never again."

Daniel caught a glimmer of regret and a pinch of blame in the gaze Gabe gave him before pivoting around to walk on. Daniel knew it wasn't imagined. Gabe blamed him for dragging Jade into this life. And Daniel felt pretty much the same. But it couldn't be helped. Daniel stifled a curse as he straightened his shoulders and followed Gabe.

From the moment he'd showed up at Gabe's house months ago, Daniel regretted ever allowing Jade to get mixed up with solving the mystery of his father's death. If he'd left her at home instead of trying to bargain with her for the keys to her family's boat, Jade would still be safe. Gabe and his brothers would never have been separated from their parents. But Daniel's father had always taught him one thing about having regrets. Regretting something only meant you didn't intend to fix it. Daniel, though, knew now deep in his gut he'd fix this for them. After they left Uukin, he'd risk his life to return Jade and her brothers home. Even if it meant losing her forever. He loved her too much to drag her down the inevitable path of death he was traveling.

Daniel rubbed his hand along the dirt walls of the tunnel. Pensively, he dug out a rock, turned around and tossed it. Maybe what his father wanted him to do was impossible. Rayne wasn't able to change his life without signing a death certificate. Why would anything be different for him or even Nickel? Faulk was a fool to drop out of flight school to try to reconcile things between their family. And Daniel was a fool to let him. It didn't matter, he and Faulk knew he was a selfish bastard. That, may not ever change.

"You coming or what?" Gabe called.

10

Faulk didn't stop staring at Michael. He didn't trust him. Never did. Faulk sat quietly and bit his nail. The stink from the tunnel no longer bothered him. But the hatred coming from Michael did. It scared him. And lately, ever since he'd left Flight School to reconcile with Daniel, he'd been scared a lot. Showing it wouldn't help since his cousin didn't think much of him anyway.

Nickel slid closer to him, then whispered, "Why did you take it from him?"

Faulk shrugged when Michael pivoted away from them to lean against the wall of the cave and tossed his knife next to a rock buried in the dirt. "I had a good reason."

Nickel gawked. "You are crazy. Do you know what Michael is?" Both his eyebrows lifted.

"A Zukar – a master thief. Just like your father and Daniel." Faulk bent his leg. "So what? I'm not impressed."

"Michael's not just a Zukar, he's on the cleanse team. They go out and kill off any threat to the snatch job." Nickel dropped his face in his hands and shook his head from side to side, then croaked, "He likes killing people."

Faulk smirked. "I knew there was a reason I didn't get along with him."

Leaning in closer, Nickel added, "It doesn't matter. Just give him what he wants so he'll let us go."

"For a kid, you sure act like you know more than I do about this." Faulk spit out the fingernail he'd bitten off. "And I'm smart enough to know, if he lets us go, it'll be because he's killed us."

Nickel jabbed Faulk with his elbow and whispered, "Michael's like a brother to Daniel and me. But you don't understand. Even if he hates us, he will take care of us. It's the Zukar code. You wouldn't know because you didn't grow up with my dad."

Faulk snorted. "No I didn't grow up with your father around. And that's why I ditched my graduation from flight school to find you. But I'm not my father. I know Uncle Rayne and my dad didn't get along and couldn't forgive each other's differences. I'm sticking with you and Daniel whether you want me to or not." He nodded in Michael's direction. "Michael and the Zukars you were loyal to don't really care about you. Gabe and Michael might pretend, but they don't *want* what's best for *us*. They want to use us for what's best for them."

"I, uh…" confusion marred Nickel's features, "I don't understand."

"You remember the promise we made to each other when we saved your home planet, Merwin, from being blown up?"

"Uh-hum."

"We promised we would never look back. That we would help people…save people instead of hurting them or stealing from them." Faulk swallowed. "But Gabe, Franz and Michael…" he shook his head, "they don't want that. At least from where I'm sitting."

"That's a lie. We grew up together. They are Zukar brothers to Daniel and me and want to stay with us. Anyway, we left that behind when we ran from Merwin." Nickel grimaced.

"They might want to stay with us, but they don't want to change sides like us." Faulk's gaze looked sternly at Nickel. "Remember what your father stood for when he turned away from the Zukar and stole the Pakeet that changed our lives? He was making a change from the life of a murderer and thief—and he wanted you both to do the same. Are you forgetting that? Are you turning your back on the promise we made to each other for friends that hate me—your own blood?"

Nickel gulped, and answered quietly, "No."

"What we are going to do is…just play along. Michael needs us to find the thing I stole from him and if he wants it, he'll deliver us alive, to Daniel." Faulk smirked, knowing he could play this game out for as long as possible if he had too.

"You really think that is going to work?" Nickel sighed and laid his head against the dirt.

"No, but I hope so. It's the only plan I've got." And this plan was about as bad as dropping out of Flight School to rekindle his relationship with his estranged uncle and cousins. The dream of convincing his father to make up with his brother and for them to be a big happy family totally blew up in his face. How ever it played out, it no longer mattered. Faulk would make this right. One way or another. And despite Michael wanting to kill him, he would survive – he hoped.

Michael's stare landed on Faulk. "That's enough rest." He tapped the butt of his gun on his palm. "Let's move."

"Are we going to meet Daniel?" Nickel asked, cautiously.

Michael studied Faulk's face. "No, it's better if we keep going to a place where I can deal with your brother on my terms." He spit on the dirt floor. "And if he's as good a Zukar as he father bragged he is, he'll survive and keep up. But if he doesn't, I've got a back-up plan that just might get rid of two of my problems."

Faulk closed his eyes. His heart sank in his chest and he bit back a groan. They were so dead, and he knew the stupid flight school hadn't prepared him for this—his possible death.

11

Daniel knew something was off. For Michael to 'rescue' Faulk and Nickel but not signal to them went against all their training. He'd promised Bry, Jade's father, he'd protect her, but for some reason, Daniel had an inner itch that told him it wasn't just Jade who needed protecting. The clue he found weighed heavy in his pocket. But he hoped it wasn't what the nagging voice in his head taunted.

The tunnel was dank and dark but Daniel still tried to search around for some clue or sign that what his gut was telling him was wrong. Nickel would've left something behind to let him know which way they were going—unless Michael didn't allow him to. If that was the case, then why wouldn't Michael follow Zukar protocol? None of it made sense. The truth was, ever since they'd left Merwin, Michael was acting strange.

Daniel considered Michael the quiet type since he'd never seemed to want to hang out with the rest of them, and when he did, Michael always ignored them. Gabe constantly said his brother was different when Daniel wasn't around, but Daniel didn't believe it. Daniel just hoped he'd get to Michael and Faulk before they started fighting because there was no way Faulk would back down, or Michael wouldn't beat Faulk to a pulp if given the chance.

He caught up to Gabe and Jade who were standing up ahead. They were looking at the hole they planned to climb up to get out of the tunnels.

"About time you caught up." Gabe's lighthearted chuckle echoed.

Daniel crossed his arms in front of his chest. "Something's up with Michael. The clues I found on our way just seem off." Daniel knew bringing up something about Michael was taking a big chance. Gabe and his brothers were fiercely protective of each other – even against Daniel, whom Gabe considered one of them.

Gabe got serious, his expression shuttering closed and the hardness Daniel knew lurked beneath the surface flickered. "What you saying?"

"Yeah, what are you saying?" Jade repeated, confusion marring her features. "You know Michael would never do anything to sabotage what we plan on doing here."

Daniel's frown softened. He didn't need Jade getting any more defensive than she already was. "Bry and my father taught us to have a meet-up spot if the snatch team got separated. Why would Michael save Faulk and Nickel, then not meet us in the tunnels where it's safe?" He lifted a gold ring with an emerald shaped like the letter *F*. "This is Faulk's. A gift from his father and he never takes it off. Why did I find it wedged in the dirt wall?"

Gabe stepped to him, his face angry. "I don't know, maybe he dropped it. But I do know I don't like what the hell you're implying."

"I don't care what you like. I just want my brother and my cousin with me." Daniel hit his chest with his open palm. "Admit it! Michael's been actin' strange ever since we met up on Merwin."

"Strange? I don't think so." Gabe's chin tilted up at Daniel. "You and he never got along anyway."

His muscles got taut and he stepped forward. "No, we haven't but it doesn't explain to me why my cousin left a ring like a warning. Like—"

Gabe punched Daniel in the jaw. "Don't you say another damn word about my brother!"

"Stop it!" Jade screeched.

Daniel cut a glance her way and sucked his bleeding bottom lip into his mouth. His hand came up to rub his jaw. "I'll let that one go. But if I find out that your brother isn't with us – that he's holding Faulk and Nickel just to piss me off, I'll deal with him – my way."

"And I'll deal with you in mine – friend." Gabe spat on the ground.

Jade sighed. "Can we just relax a minute? Maybe they had to move. Something could've been after them, don't you think? Michael wouldn't do something like take them with him unless he had a good reason."

Daniel frowned. "You don't know Michael like I do. He's different when he's not around ya'll." He wanted to take the words back as soon as they'd left his lips. It was too late.

Gabe stepped forward again as if he was ready to do battle. Daniel didn't back down, his fist balled and his breathing was slow and steady. Although Gabe was his friend, he really wanted to kick someone's butt. Right now he was so frustrated with this so called mission and it's mishaps.

Jade slipped between them. "What do you mean?"

"I've cleaned up after some of the jobs he's done. I've seen him at work, and Michael can be ruthless. And well," Daniel pivoted away from them, "we've had more than one argument about it."

Jade expelled a breath. "Are you saying that Michael and you argued? Fought? About what—a snatch job?" She rested her hands on her hips. "That's not a big deal."

"Not just a job, but the way he acted on one. Specifically…" He didn't want to tell them what he'd witness on his last job with Michael. The one that made him think twice about pairing up with Gabe's older brother ever again. "Specifically something he did to an innocent bystander."

Jade appeared visibly shaken. Then whispered, "Tell me."

"Enough of this shit!" Gabe stepped between them. "You don't tell her nothing. What happens on the snatch job stays there. Got it?" His stare quarreled with Daniel's.

"I won't. But you know what I'm talkin' about. You remember what I told you about that job. And I want to make sure I can trust him not to repeat it – not to do that to my brother or my cousin."

"Guys I'm standing right here! Stop-leaving-me out!" Jade stomped.

Gabe and Daniel faced off. "I said, enough," Gabe ground out, seemingly jarred by Jade's outburst.

"For now." Daniel shut his eyes against the sad expression on Jade's face.

Gabe turned away from them and proceeded to climb up the open cracks in the tunnel. But Daniel didn't budge.

"Why would you blame Michael for keeping Nickel away from you?" Jade's hoarse whisper was teased with pain. "He's my brother and he's only ever showed me that he cared for us – even you. My father makes sure we treat you and Nickel as if you were our family by blood."

"Because I know my cousin well enough that there's no way he would've left something like this behind without a good reason." Daniel rocked back on his heels.

"My brother wouldn't do that. Nickel is like our family. Michael used to play with him, and you." She swallowed. "Is this because of me? Because I messed up and we aren't together?"

Daniel reached out to her, and she stepped back. He hated seeing her like this, hurt with tears building up in her eyes. "Don't do that, okay? It's got nothing to do with us. The way I feel about being with you. To me, we are together – just you don't realize that yet. And the deal with Michael and me—give it time, the truth will come out. It always does." He tugged her into his arms and she struggled. "Shhh, hey, shhh," Daniel soothed.

Jade couldn't stop the tears from falling. She sniffled. "This is my fault, Daniel. If Nickel wouldn't have gotten taken – you wouldn't be blaming Michael now for it. Especially, when you really should blame me for this mess."

Daniel's heart was throbbing in his chest. He'd really messed things up with her. "Kiss. Can I kiss you?" he whispered. Jade hesitated and started to pull away. "Please Jade, I need to kiss you." Daniel didn't wait for her denial again; he gently touched his lips to hers. And his heart relaxed, his chest swelled next to hers and he stifled a sob. He couldn't believe she didn't know how much he needed her to save him. To ground him and make him want to do the right thing – for all of them.

Whimpering, Jade pressed her palms against his chest. "This is it Daniel. I—" she stammered hoarsely, "it hurts too much to go back and forth like this with you. I know you are going to tell me that you aren't angry with me. Or you made a mistake when you accused me of Nickel's kidnapping. But it seems to me that you are determined to point blame at someone. And since you want me—just as much as you are angry with me, you figure saying that Michael is now to blame is okay. I just…we can't keep doing this."

His finger lifted her chin. "I'm-not-letting-you go. Listen to me."

"No! You listen to me now. This has to stop. You have to stop pulling me closer to you and then saying and doing things that push me away. Blaming Michael—my brother—of doing something to

Nickel or Faulk is just…" Jade jerked out of his grasp, "wrong. And this friendship ends. I…there's no way this can work. I'm…my feelings for you are all mixed up. It hurts." Tears fell unchecked from her eyes. "You are no longer my friend." She rushed away from him and started climbing after Gabe.

Daniel waited there a moment, willing himself not to be the weak man he'd once accused his father of, but it didn't work, tears fell. He'd lost them all, Jade and his family—and part of him knew that even the friendship that he'd grown up with as a surrogate family may also fall apart. With a final deep breath, he angrily wiped away his stray tears and climbed out of the hole.

12

Daniel stomped on a brown rock. Sprouts of copper colored grass stuck out of the charred terrain. Though they'd walked in silence for about a quarter mile, Daniel knew Gabe was no longer angry about his accusations. But Jade still was. She barely uttered two words to him unless it had to do with directions about the job. He didn't blame her, but he'd hoped she wouldn't make winning her back too hard.

He caught up to Gabe. "So what do we have ahead of us?"

"Don't know. Franz shut down our coms so that means he's spooked about something." Gabe slapped a long dreaded braid out of his face. "But we should be okay."

"What about Michael?" Daniel stated this question about Michael knowing it might tick Gabe off but not caring.

"He'll know what to do, he spent most of the trip over here studying anything he could about the place." Gabe cut a glance at Daniel, a ticked off edge to it. "It's expected, when prepping for a job this big. Breaking into a prison planet isn't like our other jobs."

"When's the last time you talked to Bry?" Daniel hoped the change of subjects would loosen Gabe back up.

Gabe's expression tightened. "Not since we left."

"He was supposed to meet up with us, you know? He told me so before we left." Daniel had been concerned when he'd made several calls to Bry's ships and even his home but got no response. He was sure Franz had also, but Michael told them he'd been in contact with his father and everything was fine.

"That so?" Gabe grimaced. "Something's not right."

"No, it's not. But I did want you to know I brought it up to Michael on the ship." Daniel studied Gabe's face while they were walking. He hoped his revelation wouldn't test their friendship further. "It was before we argued last time. I asked him what happened when he was with the Sira Zukar." Daniel knew the name of the king of the thieves would make Gabe consider his concerns. At least he hoped so, because something was bugging him and he wanted Gabe with him on it.

"What'd he say?" His response was stilted as though it bothered him to even touch on the possibilities.

"Michael said it was none of my damn business. That it was his family and that I had enough to worry about with my own worthless cousin and weak kid brother." Daniel cleared his throat. "And he mentioned speaking to your father. He confirmed all was well and your dad was in hiding somewhere that Michael felt he didn't need to tell me."

A low growl erupted. "What are you sayin' exactly?"

"Just listen, without the growl. You haven't talked to your parents since we left. Michael and Franz were the only ones who talked to the Sira Zukar, and Franz was barely breathing when we put him on the ship to cure him." Daniel remembered seeing Franz being carried by

Michael and Franz appeared to be near death. Michael had only looked slightly better.

"I know. I figured they didn't want to talk about it. Just 'cause it was something they weren't ready to talk about."

"When we meet up with him, we need to ask some questions. We can't break into the cage if we aren't working as a team. The Warden will kill us." Daniel stared ahead at Jade several feet in front of them. "All of us – and what he'd do to Jade…unspeakable torture."

"I know. I'll handle him okay." Gabe conceded. "I don't even want to think of the ways my father's going to beat me when he finds out we brought Jade on a job like this. I'll be lucky to still be alive."

"Yeah, I think he'll knock me out first. He did tell me to take care of his daughter before we left." Daniel patted his back. "Then he made me take ya'll with us."

"So, Jade and you really over?" Gabe sounded a bit skeptical.

"She says so. But I'm not giving up." Daniel never would. He'd known Jade since she was born. Ever since he could remember, he had a soft spot for her. Maybe because her brothers ignored her and he felt bad for her, seeing how hard she fought for their attention – for his attention. He'd never thought in a million years that his feelings were beyond that of a pseudo big brother. But when Faulk showed an interest in her, and then Jade, out of the blue, kissed Daniel on her birthday, Daniel had never thought of himself as her big brother again.

Gabe released a chuckle. "You never did know when to let go."

"I have no problems letting go." Daniel looked at the setting moon and wondered when, or if, this place had ever seen daylight. They'd been there two days and nothing close to sun had peeked out of the horizon. "A lot of girls came and went before your sister. So-called friends too."

Gabe snorted. "The girls never really left. I don't remember you ever telling one of them it was officially over. So, as far as I know, you left behind at least twenty girls on Merwin who probably still think they have a chance at manipulating that heart of yours back into their little traps."

"And you don't?" Daniel laughed out loud. "But they don't matter to me." He toyed with the necklace heavy on his chest. Its beads reminded him of the one female besides Jade who had held his heart: his mother. She'd made the gift for him the year she died. His heart would never forget her. And the beads calmed him. "I didn't want to hurt their feelings by telling them I was bored. So I just—avoided. Like most guys do."

"You made avoiding an art. And what happened to me when you 'avoided' was I got bombarded with questions referring your whereabouts. Information I wouldn't be the one to give out." He winked at Daniel and elbowed him.

"I covered for you too. Don't act like you are innocent. I can't remember how many times I took on extra work on a job because you didn't show up due to some female persuasion." He grinned.

"Yeah, my dad always warned me a woman would be the one to lead me astray. He was right, the last job we did, one of the girls tried to lure me off watch." He bent to pick up a prickly gray rock and tossed it up in the air.

"But I stopped you," Daniel scoffed. "And she wasn't even that pretty in the face."

"Beauty can be in a great body too, you know." Gabe winked. "Besides, who said I had to look into her face for what I wanted to do to her?"

Daniel raised an eyebrow. "If you say so." He hated this place. No birds flew, no animals roamed with the exception of one of the plump beetles that thrived in this dry and barren land. The land beneath their feet was even heated, felt like they were walking on hot rocks. The only light was from the overly large moon that cast a gold glow across the lands.

"I miss them, you know. My dad and mom…I'm worried about them. But I didn't want to tell my brothers." Gabe kept a watchful eye on Jade who was up ahead of them. "How do you do it? How do you deal with having no one? Your mother and father both gone. I never told you how sorry I was that Rayne died."

"Thanks for mentioning it. Not having my mother—I thought I was used to it. But I never was. When my father got killed, I was screwed up. Part of me still hated him for becoming weak. When he'd turned away from the life of a Zukar, he just seemed bent on finding himself, and me. If I didn't have Nickel to think about, things would be different for me—I wouldn't be here." He swallowed the guilt that still sat heavily in his chest. "I ruined our last days together by hating my father. For not realizing I loved him deeper, for caring enough about me to want to risk his life for mine, for wanting to make my life better." Daniel hoped raising Nickel the way his father would've wanted would help him at least feel as though he'd become the man his father wanted him to be. Even though some would believe that leaving the life of a Zukar could be easy, it wasn't. Most never turned away from the Zukar way of life and lived to speak about it. Because of Daniel's father, at least he and Nickel could prove history wrong. They had escaped that life, left Merwin behind before they could be thrown in jail, or killed by the Zukar traitor rituals. "I'll never forgive myself for hurting him like I did."

"I see that. My father seemed to want us to change too. At least when he sent us with you. For him to send Jade with you, that was a clue he wasn't telling us everything."

"No, Bry and my father both wanted the same things for us. The problem was your father had to protect his family. He helped my father by throwing off Haden and the Sira Zukar, making them think that maybe he was a traitor to the Zukar by stealing the Pakeet from my father. But Haden figured out that your father didn't know where it was. He knew my father had stolen the treasure and hid it from them."

"So, now where does that put us? If we come here and free the Zukar who've been imprisoned, will that get the Sira Zukar and the King of Merwin off our backs so we can go home?" Gabe groaned. "I hope so."

"I don't know. But I do know that ever since Nickel and I were on the run from the King of Merwin, I wanted to spit in his face by freeing the innocents he had put in prison here." Angrily, Daniel's finger pointed to the ground. "Right here where he tried to put me and Nickel after our father was murdered by Haden. And the Sira Zukar—he never liked my dad either. My father mentioned that the Sira Zukar tried to have him killed on several occasions since he thought my father was a threat to his rule over the Zukar."

Gabe smirked. "He was right. No one liked the Sira Zukar. Up until your father stopped leading the complex jobs, everyone listened to him over the Sira Zukar. That's why Haden wanted him dead."

"True. True. I didn't see that coming though." Daniel felt the tease of anger at Haden's betrayal. He flexed his hands into fists to numb it.

"He told everyone you were Haden's protégé. Too bad he wanted to kill you since he considered competition best dead."

Daniel scoffed. "Thanks for that—friend."

"Don't say I didn't try to warn you about him. I never liked the guy."

"I know." Daniel noticed Jade had stopped walking. "But I wouldn't put it past the Sira Zukar and the King of Merwin to be working together for some gain. It was rumored that there was a discount to be had on the energy mined here on Uukin for slave labor. I wouldn't doubt that the Sira Zukar tipped the King of Merwin off about possible prisoners. It would explain why a small number of Zukar kids went missing so soon after their parents were killed or disappeared." Daniel spotted Jade's aggressive stance ahead of them. It nagged at him and he left Gabe behind to run up behind her.

"Stop!" Jade yelled. Her face filled with fear. "Look."

Daniel stared past her and his jaw locked. The ground beyond where they stood was cracked and broken. Large faults, caused either by an earthquake or underground movement separated the ground by several dozen feet. On the edge of each crevice, pointed tips of rock were covered in a slimy green substance. For miles there were fragmented lines of nothing but air separating the dirtlike platforms.

"Damn." Daniel sighed.

"What the hell?" Gabe said from behind him.

"There is no way we can make it across here without breaking something." Jade picked up a rock and dropped it into the crack in front of her.

Daniel raised his wrist timer and counted the seconds before the rock hit the surface below. "About 368ft deep."

"Ideas?" Jade avoided eye contact with Daniel.

"Do you think Michael figured out a way around these?" Daniel asked.

Gabe swung back his ponytail riddled with dreaded braids and beads. "He probably stayed underground." He hit a fist into his palm. "I should've thought of that. We're too far to backtrack."

"I know. Only one thing to do now," Daniel stated.

Jade smirked. "Jump?"

"You got it." Daniel tapped his forehead with his finger. "Glad to know you remember how I think."

"Jump!" Gabe shook his head. "I don't know. Do you realize that each edge of those things have poisonous slime on them? It looks like some kind of animal made those cracks."

"What's the risk? Looks like we don't have a choice, so let's just do this thing." Daniel chuckled. "I'll go first, then Jade, then you." Inside his heart thudded loudly. The jump was dangerous. It was wide with an endless bottom waiting for them if they missed. He couldn't dwell on the negative possibilities or he'd cause his own demise – along with the others.

Jade raised her hand. "Uh, Jade standing right here. I have an idea."

Daniel moved closer to her. "Let's hear it." He made sure he moved within her personal space, his arm brushed against hers, but she held her ground and attempted to ignore him.

"I have some netting in my bag. It may be able to act like a safety net." Jade slid off her backpack and searched around inside.

"How far does yours go?" Daniel eyed her, swallowing back the itch to tell her it wouldn't work.

She stared at Daniel's mouth, then her eyes fluttered back up to his. "About twenty feet."

Daniel released a heavy breath. "That might work the first couple of gaps." He pulled a small tube from the device around his ear, adjusted the base of it and a 3D screen appeared. With a twist of his fingers, the small image zoomed forward and sprouted white numbers between each crack. "That'll work the first two jumps. After that, we're going commando."

13

Daniel paced several feet. Jade had sprung her net and it even took her two tries to get it to latch on to the other side of the huge crevice. The darkness of night was a blessing and a curse. It covered their presence but also made it difficult to see what lie ahead of them. "Remember, don't look down," he told Jade who was walking backwards next to him.

"I'm fine. Please, don't worry about me. This isn't the first time I've been put to the test, you know." Irritation laced Jade's voice.

"I know, but you aren't a seasoned Zukar. You only went on one job with me and that was under six months ago." Daniel hated to bring it up, but this was like the last treasure hunt they went on. It could kill her. Jumping across a ravine wasn't the safest route.

She snorted. "Whatever."

Daniel reached out to touch her and she jerked her arm away. "You'll be okay. And if you fall, you know I'll catch you." Without a backwards glance, Daniel rocketed off. His arms pumped. Breath poured into his lungs rapidly in and out. He jumped. No thoughts, just pure adrenaline pumped through him. "Ahhhhhhhh!"

Landing with a few inches to spare, he rolled forward to soften the fall. His mouth formed an O as he let out the breath. Then he jumped up and whooped. "What – a – rush!"

He needed it – the thrill, the blood pumping through his veins. It reminded him that as long as he lived, he had a chance to make the things he'd left undone with his father right.

"Step back! Jade's on her way." Gabe called.

Daniel braced himself. Hunched forward, he extended a hook from his belt and pressed the small button its side. The hook sprang out, attached to a rope secured at his belt and pierced the ground. He gave it a pull and crouched ready to catch Jade if he had to.

Jade ran towards him, her legs lunged forward with arms circling, she hurled herself through the air. Daniel caught her and they rolled back just in the middle of the first jump. Unfortunately there would be another one after this. He moved out the way as Gabe followed.

Bending to give Jade a hand, he said, "That was the easiest one."

"I know and it sucked." Gabe shook his head. "The stuff on the edges looks nasty, and smells. It's poisonous."

Daniel retracted his hook. "Don't go to the edge to take off the net. The poison won't let you bend over it."

"I have a rag I can lie down on and get the netting off," she answered and started to walk over to the side of the fault.

"Hold up." Daniel pulled her back. "Don't, I can't risk you getting poisoned. We don't know what that stuff does to you. It's not worth it."

She gave him a wry smile and nodded. "Whatever you say." Then she placed her hand on his. "I want to do this for you and Nickel. I won't make it harder on us to save them okay—but I don't think Michael is doing anything wrong. He's just protecting them and he'll meet up with us where it's safe."

Daniel bit his tongue. He wanted to believe her, but his gut was telling him different. The heavy ring of Faulk's in his pocket wasn't a fluke; it had to be a call for help. It was a risk Faulk took, since it was possible they wouldn't have gone into the caves, but it was the best possible place for him to find Faulk's clue.

"I hope so," Daniel whispered sincerely.

Gabe came up and slapped Daniel on the back. "Ready for the next jump?"

"Sure as rain. One down—two more to go." Daniel was ready. Only thing was, watching Jade jump it was starting to get to him, making him feel helpless. Daniel retracted the hook on his belt. Eyeing the distance of the next jump, his body tensed. He felt a tremble. The ground under his feet was moving. Rocks jumbled past him.

"Jade!" Daniel stepped forward. Bracing Jade against his chest as she staggered, he caught her before she fell.

Her hands were braced on his chest. "What is it?"

"Sounds like a small earthquake." Gabe relaxed when the tremors ceased.

Daniel released a breath. "It's done—for now."

"I don't know." Jade rubbed her fingers together, something she'd always done when she was uncomfortable. "Maybe I…"

Daniel grabbed her hand. "We'll be okay. Just follow my lead. Only two more jumps to go."

The second jump went well. Daniel made it first and the other two followed. It was closer than the first rift. It was riddled with pointed and jagged rocks positioned to impale a person of less skill. Daniel hated that the jumps were getting harder, not knowing Jade's skill at this type of challenge made him cautious – more than he was used to being. He stood with his hands on his hips and studied the next drop, which was glowing slightly from the golden shine of the moon that never seemed to move.

Jade placed her hands on her hips. "Why are we waiting?"

Daniel glanced at her and forced his eyes away. He missed her and the easy conversation they'd had on the ship. The playing and horsing around they did now seemed like a distant memory. He was at odds and didn't know how to approach her, didn't want to give her the space she desired because he was afraid if he did so – she'd never come back to him. Daniel knew it was selfish to feel that way. So he said nothing.

Jade's hand touched his arm, he fought to stop himself from touching her back. Putting her on tighter guard around him was the last thing he wanted to do. "I'm waiting for the tremors to stop. They're slight, but I still feel them." Daniel didn't want to tell her what he was really concerned about. The tremors were occurring closer together, and he was counting them, hoping to find a rhythm and the precise time to jump that would ensure they'd all survive.

"Man, it's not letting up." Gabe's rich voice didn't hold his usual jovial tone.

Daniel hated to admit it but even Gabe sounded worried. They passed an understanding stare between them. "I'm counting it."

"Me too." Gabe chewed his bottom lip. "Sucks."

"What's it telling you?" Jade stepped in front of Daniel.

"That waiting isn't gonna make it better," Daniel stated. "I'm going first again."

"I want to go last this time," Jade responded.

Daniel wanted to argue with her but Gabe shook his head no. Daniel nodded at Gabe's silent warning to concede to Jade's input. "That's fine. I'll be there to catch you." Every muscle in him was screaming to disagree with her, but he was going to back down—this time.

Gabe didn't wait to warn them, he jumped. His back tensed as he arched, barely making it past the poisonous sides of the edge. Stumbling a bit he fell forward on his outstretched hands.

Another tremor hit. The ground moved so fiercely that Jade toppled back into Daniel. He held her close a moment. "Jade, you sure you don't want to go next?" He should let her go, but he didn't. His arm stayed wrapped around her waist.

She wouldn't look at him, but kept her hazel eyes averted in Gabe's direction. "Daniel, I'm fine. Can't you just stop acting like I can't think on my own? Even on the ship when I'd want us to sneak off – away from my brothers – you kept reminding me of the consequences. I don't need anymore reminders."

"I know, but I had to. You know I didn't see you as incompetent? I just wanted to protect you, not because of our previous friendship, but because that's what a guy who's in love is supposed to do." He didn't want her to think things were over between them. And he couldn't resist planting a kiss on her forehead. "You've always been my friend. But now, and forever, you're more to me than that Jade— you help keep it together. You helped me make my father's dream for me real."

"How?" Her voice came out husky with emotion, and her eyes watered. "I still miss him so much."

"Me too, but you helped me by going with me to find the pakeet. His treasure—the one that changed his life. He bargained the only thing he'd known to be—a Zukar, a thief, a murderer—with his life for that treasure because he hoped I wouldn't want to become like he was. He wanted me to be better. He wanted me to save lives, make things right, instead of destroying everyone I touched for my own purpose. And I blew it—I spat at him because I wanted to stay true to the Zukar ways."

"You didn't know." Jade's coffee brown hand caressed his cheek.

"I knew," he replied hoarsely, unable to conceal the depths of his guilt and self-disgust. "But I didn't care. Jade...you, you make me believe I can do this. That I can change for him, for me—and for you."

Jade smiled with an itch of remorse in its depths. "You can't do it for me Daniel, you have to do it for yourself – you've got to know that you are worthy and able to change." She shook her head. "I'm still trying to figure out my own way, and I keep messing it up. Even you pointed that out. I can't help you any more than I can help myself—but I have to be honest with myself. If I continue to be your girlfriend, I'll hide behind you and never figure out who I can be by myself."

"But…" Daniel wanted to plead with her.

Jade put a finger to his mouth. "Give me time to figure this out. My heart has always been yours—will forever be yours. But I need the time to learn if I can do it, if I can be the person I've always wanted to be. And you love me too much to give me the freedom to do it. So I have to take the risk that you'll still love me when I've taken the time to become the best I can be for you." She pulled his face down to kiss him.

"Keep it moving people!" Gabe hollered.

Daniel nibbled her lower lip, then devoured them as if he was starving and whispered between deepening the kiss, "I love you."

She smiled and broke the kiss. "I know. Now go. I'll make the jump, and I know you'll be on the other side waiting for me."

Even though his gut told him he shouldn't leave her, he did. Daniel ran at high speed, then leaped through the air to the next rocky platform where Gabe waited.

He missed the mark. Falling. The air hit his face and he scrambled to grasp anything he could reach. Gabe tossed down a rope. Daniel's heart hammered in his chest, and he grasped the rope on the first attempt. But instead of the rope retracting like it was supposed to, it slackened, pummeling him down several more feet before it became taunt.

"Pull it up!" Daniel hollered at Gabe.

Gabe peered over the side of the cliff-like edge to the rift. "It's stuck! You'll have to climb up, but don't touch the sides of this thing—it's got poison all over it."

"No kidding," Daniel muttered, and held the rope steady to avoid the splattering of green slime on the sides of the crevice wall. He shimmied up the rope a few feet when it jerked and pulled him up. Thankfully the edges weren't blanketed in the stuff; there were splotches of dried rock, and Daniel was able to balance himself with his foot as he climbed.

"Here." Gabe's hand shot out to grab Daniel's, careful not to step in the goo.

Daniel found a dry spot on the side of the crevice and pulled himself up with the hand Gabe extended him. He threw the rope down and pivoted around to stare in Jade's direction. "Damn!" and another tremor hit.

He and Gabe held up their hands to tell Jade to wait to jump.

"Why the hell did you tell me to let her go last?" Daniel spat out the words in a growl.

"I didn't know, man. I thought it would work out." Gabe paced behind Daniel on the large platform.

The ground continued to shake and Jade appeared as though she was fighting for balance.

"The one she's on is being hit harder." Daniel searched his mind for a way out of this. "She's gonna have to jump anyway. The ground she's on is crumbling." He felt helpless. Daniel tugged on the rope at his waist, hoping it would hold both him and Jade if it had to. "Brace yourself in case I have to get her!"

"Done!" Gabe confirmed.

Jade ran forward and leaped.

Daniel's heartbeat froze in his chest. Chanting a prayer his mother used when he was younger, he hoped she'd make the jump. He lunged, arms outstretched to catch her. But she just missed the edge of the cliff.

"Ugh!" Daniel grabbed her by the wrist. Gabe grabbed him by a rope at his waist.

"Daniel!" Jade screamed and kicked her legs in the air, her hands slipping on the edge.

He was bent over, just clear of a spot of poison slime on the edge of the cliff. "Don't touch the slime."

"I'm—trying-not-to-fall!" her eyes filled with fear and she squirmed.

"Stop moving! Hold on," Daniel hollered.

Gabe grunted and pulled at Daniel's waist. "Don't drop her."

"I-won't." Daniel tugged at Jade's flailing form while dragging her up over the edge of the cliff.

"Oww!" Jade cringed as the jagged rock covered in slime on the edge of the cliff tore through her clothes. Blood spilled freely from the gnashed on her skin. Green goo covered her exposed skin and within seconds Jade went limp.

Daniel gave her one last pull and laid her on the ground. His body shook as he stomped at the ground and he let out sob mixed roar. "No!"

14

Jade's limp body was sprawled over Daniel. Quiet regretful tears fell from his eyes.

"Hey." Gabe tapped Jade's relaxed face. "Jade. Wake up, wake up," his voice cracked.

Daniel ripped off the soiled portion of her vest that rode low on her stomach. He tossed it over the side of the cliff. The never setting moon taunted him with its yellowed hue that cast a golden glow on the black, cracked ground. Trees with blood-red trunks and green leaves covered the expanse ahead.

Daniel jerked, feeling her stir. "Jade, baby, talk to me."

She groaned, her eyes remained closed and she mumbled softly to herself as if in a dream.

"We have to take cover, you know." Gabe gave a furtive glance around. "We're in a place Franz hasn't had a chance to fully secure yet."

"I know." Daniel lifted Jade into his arms while Gabe grasped her backpack. "Let's move. At least…she's still alive."

They walked in silence for a while. Daniel held Jade firmly as her body thrashed about. He tightened his hold when she'd calmed down, only to start up again. Stumbling as her back bowed, and Jade's eyes rolled back into her head as her teeth chattered, Daniel whispered to her. Daniel forced his thumb between her lips to push her tongue down and mouth open to prevent her from swallowing her tongue. Her fevered skin burned against his, but Daniel adjusted her smaller body against his cool leather vest.

"How much further until the next possible meeting point with Michael?" Daniel asked with disgust.

With each passing moment, his anger at Michael grew. If he hadn't grown up with Michael, he doubted he'd be able to stomach Michael's typical hateful nature. Even though Michael was always the brutal one of Gabe's brothers, Daniel had to admit that the guy loved his family— in his own way. He couldn't help being angry at Michael for leading him and Gabe on this chase behind him when they had come here for a different purpose.

His concern over Jade's injury made him walk faster and rejuvenated his angry muscles. They had to get to the safety of the trees if they wanted to rest and take care of her.

"The tree line isn't that far now. But…" Gabe's voice came out broken. "What if we can't get her to wake up? What if it nothing works?"

"The leaves on those trees can be mashed with some of the herbs I have in my pack to wake her up." Daniel hoped he was right. His heart was beating so fast in his chest, his blood felt like it was on fire. To lose Jade this way teased the already stabbing pain within him deeper. This wasn't the way things were supposed to end. He'd set about re-writing his story.

If they got through this, he'd make better decisions. The price of this misadventure was too high. Jade was never supposed to get hurt.

Nickel and Faulk being taken wasn't part of the plan. Most of all Michael's renegade move didn't seem obvious until now. The reasons for this mission didn't seem as important if it could mean failure and more loss. If they didn't get off this planet alive, he'd never forgive himself for dragging her into this mess. And Gabe wouldn't either. His friend and he had been like brothers, but something like this could sever his friendship for good.

"I hope so…I hope so." Gabe sounded worried and a bit doubtful.

They'd finally made it to the copse of trees, and within minutes were thrown into darkness as the moon that had hung in the sky for the two days of their journey dipped beneath the copper clouds.

Daniel held a wrestling Jade tighter while Gabe prepared a place to for them to lie by sweeping discarded leaves and debris together to place her on.

Gabe took the small satchel off Daniel's hip. "This should calm her fever. The waking up will have to be done when we find one of the blood red leaves. It's soft and not poisonous." Gabe held out his hands to take Jade from Daniel.

"I can't let her go." Daniel's voice deepened. "It's my fault…mine." He knelt with her and laid her out on the soft green leaves. His fingers touched the side of her face and he adjusted her head on his arm for her comfort. He leaned over and kissed her cracked lips.

"It's not your fault. We should have made her stay on the ship with Franz." Gabe stood with his hands on his hips. His long dreaded braids hung over the side of his copper vest all the way down to his form-fitted pants.

"I know." Daniel sighed.

Gabe's eyes held Daniel's. "I only need a few of the blood leaves to add to the powder you gave me to wake her. But what I have here will get the fever under control 'til then. If the mixer wakes her up, there is a side effect." Then he forced some of the powder from Daniel's satchel into Jade opened mouth as she let out a horse scream.

"What is the side effect?" Daniel asked, afraid of Gabe's answer.

"It forces her to waken from the state she's in. So if she is in the grip of a bad nightmare, she'll relive it for the first few minutes after she wakes up. Not to mention, she'll be unpredictable until the herbs calm her. It could be thirty minutes of hell—trying to fight her off."

Daniel held her tightly as she struggled in her slumber. "And from the looks of her, she's not having a good dream."

"No, she's not—but we can't wait around to see if her mood changes. We've got to keep moving. And look for the final ingredient on the way. We have to give the medicine to her soon," Gabe grumbled.

Daniel gritted his teeth and enveloped Jade in his embrace as her arms jerked about. "I can't do it if she keeps this up—the herbs will intensify her convulsions."

Gabe sat next to Daniel. "We have a bit of time for her to rest. I'll take her legs." He leaned over and held her legs down close to the ground.

"We should leave this place. Just turn around and go home as soon as we catch Michael." Daniel braced Jade's head against his arm, pried his thumb between her lips in hopes she wouldn't swallow her tongue. He was willing to throw all his hopes for this mission to the wind in order to save Jade. The mission wasn't worth it. Not anymore.

"I don't think we should give this up. I've been thinking about what you said about Michael and my parents. If there is something holding them back from returning coms to us—it can't be good. And we'd have to have something to bargain with." Gabe's expression was grave.

"Your point?" Daniel hoped this wouldn't go back to the treasure. He was done with treasure hunts, killing for hire and bargaining with men who would rather he was dead. But he waited and watched the flutter of emotions that passed on Gabe's face.

"The warden's treasure—the fire water—we can—" Gabe's eyes didn't hold the hungry anticipation of treasure hunting, they held fear.

"We can get killed going after it." Daniel closed his eyes, glad Jade's once stormy expression appeared relaxed and her breathing was steady. "I'm not using something to bargain with them—they'll sooner kill us than make a deal. You know the Sira Zukar; he'll stab us in the back, literally, after we hand over the treasure to him."

"We won't have to, the *Fanyte* and its fire-water has the power to make the one who drinks from it control the minds of men." Gabe's voice deepened. "We can use it against them just like the legend."

Daniel scoffed. "The legend also stated that the one who drinks from it will die. Go freakin' insane and die! Doesn't that defeat the purpose of controlling the minds of those who are hunting us?"

"No, it says 'One who drinks to do evil will die.' not just drinks. It's about the heart of the man or being who wields the power."

"Then I'll die. The things we've done…cannot be forgiven by the laws of the universe. My own uncle could've had us executed on Earth for being Zukar. The only reason they haven't found us is because of the masking drug we were given when we were accepted into the clan. If we steal that treasure—our hearts are already black—we are acting out of our own gain, and will die."

Gabe pointed at Daniel; anger filled his eyes. "You-don't-know that! It could help."

"No. If we continue, it is to get my brother and cousin, release the oppressed people on this planet and restore this world—like we agreed." Daniel narrowed his eyes. "Or do you and your brother's have another reason for being here?"

Gabe jerked back as if Daniel had slapped him. "What are you accusing me of again—*my friend?*" he spat.

"Nothing." Daniel didn't want to have this fight with him. Jade was too important. "Can you get the leaves for me, I think she's ready. You'll have to climb up and get the ones that don't have red veins, I have to use the ones that are bland in nutrients and they will be at the top. We have to keep giving this to her over the next few days to dull the poison until it's completely out of her system."

"Fine, I'll be back." Gabe's gait was rigid.

Daniel expelled an audible breath. His muscles were so tight he felt like he was losing it. Everything he'd known, trusted in most of his life, was falling to pieces and it all started when his father decided to change things. He wondered if things would've been different if he'd just listened to his father's ranting about leaving Merwin and living on a far-off planet where they could start over again. Daniel wiped a hand down his face and squeezed Jade closer to him. The fights he'd had with his father seemed like yesterday, and for some reason the heaviness in his heart wouldn't go away. The only times he could forget about his regret was when Jade kissed him, when he could lose himself in her and push everything away—except for the way she made him feel.

No one had ever been able to do that for him but her. The funny thing was, until she'd taken the initiative and kissed him months ago, he'd never even noticed or realized he'd felt this deeply for her. She'd accused him of hiding from her and not dealing with the unresolved issues he had with his father. Maybe she was right. But the truth was— his father was gone. Daniel would never be able to look Rayne in the face and say, "I'm sorry," he muttered out loud.

Daniel scooped up Jade. He hoped Gabe would follow as he spied the crowd of trees they entered. Scanning for the leaves they needed to wake Jade up, Daniel kept walking, periodically squeezing her thrashing form close to his chest.

Gabe slapped his back from behind. Daniel tensed as Gabe's firm hand yanked him to a stop.

Spinning around to face off with Gabe, Daniel halted.

"Here!" Gabe threw the leaves at Daniel's chest.

Daniel sunk to the hard ground, tightening his hold on Jade's slight form.

Pulling himself out of his troubled thoughts, he absently grabbed a handful of them off the ground. Then Daniel slid off his backpack. "Thanks, I..." His eyes traveled down Jade's feverish face. Her body started to tremble, her teeth chattered while in her deathly sleep.

Gabe sat crossed-legged next to them. He dug into his bag to take out a small metal box. The box was silver with a small lever on the top of its pointed edge. He pressed it. "This better work." Gabe flicked the box with his finger and said, "Turn into a bowl."

Daniel waited until the metal box reshaped itself into a bowl. Then maneuvering Jade to a comfortable position in his arms.

"Move it to the edge with your fingers," Gabe commanded the box and a surge of laser ground the leaves and herbs. The bowl shook and droplets of water it manipulated from the air dropped into its center.

Pulsating lasers mixed the contents into a soupy yellow paste.

Daniel grabbed the bowl, and used his finger to pry open Jade's shivering lips. "This is her only chance. God let this work."

Gabe massaged her throat to force her to eat. Jade went into a fit of coughing, then swallowed some. "Hold her tight!" Gabe forced the last drop into her mouth.

Jade's eyes sprang open. Her eyes were dazed and glassy. She screamed and fought against Daniel's grip. He wrapped his legs around her kicking ones and crossed her hands in front of her while trying to calm her. "Jade...shhh. It's okay, it's okay."

Gabe used his hand to wipe away the excess medicine. "It's me, your brother, Gabe."

Her eyes were wet with tears. "I don't have a brother! Who are you? Leave me alone!" She sobbed. "Please...just leave me alone."

"Hey, Jade, we want to help you. It's Daniel, remember me?" He tried to make his voice soft, like he did when she was a young girl.

She shivered, "No." Tears slid down her face as she cried, "Please let me go!" Her head jerked back with enough force to bust Daniel in the nose. Jade snaked her foot from between Daniel's legs and kneed up to hit Gabe in the chin.

Daniel grabbed his nose and lunged for Jade's shirt as she sprang from between his legs and started to run.

"Get her!" Gabe hollered and ran behind Daniel.

Jade dodged a large stone. "Leave me alone!" Eyes wild and frightened, she ducked behind a tree.

Daniel went around the side to cut her off and grabbed her, pulling her close to his chest and crossing her arms in front of her as she struggled against him.

"Jade, listen to me. We're not trying to hurt you but it's dangerous here." He spoke into her ear. "Please, relax...the side effects of the medicine we gave you should wear off soon and you'll remember."

Jade was breathing hard, trying to compose herself. "What...was...wrong with me? Confused. Jumbled, pictures. Home? Merwin? Water, where's the water? Mom!"

Gabe stepped up to her and held one of her hands. "You were poisoned when you slid off that cliff over there." He held her doubtful gaze. "I'm your brother, Gabe. We have two other brothers, Michael and Franz." His eyes watered. "I...I've been protecting you all my life—since my father put you in my arms and said, 'Jade will be this family's jewel, our treasure, because she looks like your mother' and I believed him."

She stopped her struggles against Daniel's chest. "Is this guy holding me a brother of mine?" Her eyes blinked with confusion.

Daniel cleared his throat. "No, I'm the love of your life and, your brother, Gabe's best friend." He willed Jade to relax against him, to realize he was special to her too. But she tensed.

"How do I know you're telling me the truth?" She shook her head as if trying to come out of a fog. "My head hurts and everything seems foggy."

"What do you remember?" Daniel asked, his hold on her slackened a bit. He couldn't stand the resistance he felt from her—it was breaking his heart. He wanted to say, *remember me*, but he didn't want to scare her more than she already was.

"Someplace beautiful. Water everywhere, tall green and orange-splashed trees. A little house covered in flowers. Darts—throwing darts at a tree that has a big yellow circle in the middle. Someone's holding my hand and teaching me how to toss them." Jade moved away from Daniel's chest a bit. "Then I remember a man with blond braids tickling me and throwing me up in the air. And a woman with smooth dark skin and long dark curls. She's playing a game where we slap hands and rhyme."

Gabe's voice came out gruff and broken, "Rayne, our father and Melina, our mother. You remember them."

"The boy behind you, helping you throw darts—is me," Daniel whispered and swallowed back the elation that Jade had remembered something they'd shared.

She relaxed but still moved a bit further away from him. "And I remember you, Gabe. We shared a room. But you look old, too old. Your dreadlocks are shorter, spouting from your head in different directions. We played in our room a lot. There were," Jade blinked and shifted in Daniel's arms, "beds stacked on top of each other. I slept on the top. There was a bullseye on the ceiling and I'd practice my darts there while you sang to me. Something that went like, 'And the sea of gold, those traveled of old…'"

"To the land of riches, but found…" Gabe finished with a smile on his face. "You remember me? And our home."

Jade stepped from between Daniel's arms, "Yes," and gave Gabe a hug.

Daniel bit his lip and fought not to snag her back into his arms. He waited until her reunion with Gabe ended and said her name, "Jade…do you remember me?" It came out hoarsely, even a bit pleading. Concern for where this journey would take them, how it may hurt her gnawed at him. Reminding him that he didn't deserve her—if he couldn't protect her. And hadn't. Pain—he'd caused her more than she'd ever deserved. Maybe, just maybe he should do as she asked— he should let her go.

Jade's eyes traveled from Daniel's eyes, down to his toes then back again. Her finger came up and tapped on her full wine-colored lips. "I'm sorry, I don't remember you." She lifted an eyebrow, a gesture that meant she was thinking about something important. "Did I know you long?"

He rested his hands on his hip. "Since you were born, 16 years ago."

"Really, and you're the love of my life?" Jade appeared doubtful with both eyebrows raised and her arms crossed.

Gabe chuckled. "He'd like to think so."

Daniel shot him an angry gaze. "I am," he cleared his throat, "or was."

"Hmm, I don't think you're my type. Blond, muscular, longish hair. No, not my type." She stepped closer, inspecting him further. "Were we friends? Did you bring me here to this…" Jade searched around the forest of blood red trees, and returned her gaze to his, "this place for a reason?"

"We are on the run from our Zukar brothers and sisters and the King of Merwin. I thought," Daniel flicked a gaze at Gabe, "that we were here to free some of the women and children wrongly enslaved here. But there are other things we have to take care of before we leave."

"Oh," Jade turned to face Gabe. "How long are we here for?"

"This spot," Gabe pointed downward. "About a few hours. We can't come out of this forest until the moon comes back in sight. Then we have to plan things out right since we'll be breaking into the prison territory."

"Oh." Jade followed Gabe who was making his way back to their camp. "I guess I should warm up."

Gabe grinned. "Yeah, you should." He nodded at Daniel. "Have him help you while I pack up."

Daniel walked slowly up to her. "I was the one who started you throwing darts, you know." He cautiously lifted his hand, reaching for her.

"That so? Why?" She assessed him with her eyes slanted.

Realizing she was still suspicious of him, Daniel dropped his hand. "You wanted to be the first girl Zukar to lead a job. And that's unheard of. But you would bug your brothers and me about it."

"I'd bug you?" She smiled at him, a hesitant one but one that reminded him of how they used to be.

Daniel grinned back at her. "Yeah, I didn't rough you up like your brothers did. And," he reached out a hesitant finger to touch the side of her arm, "I listened to you."

Jade glanced down at where his finger touched her. "Why would you want to?"

"I don't know, I liked to hear you talk. You always sounded excited about every new idea you came up with or the way you imagined things would be when you grew up." He went to the tree trunk where he'd given her medicine to her and handed her the backpack with her darts. "Get your darts out and I'll warm you up so that when we get out of here, you'll be able to defend yourself."

15

Michael pushed Faulk ahead of him in the dirt-covered tunnel. Daniel's stupid cousin could be the cause of his parent's death. If Faulk had never gone to Merwin to team up with Daniel, then Faulk wouldn't have been able to take the one thing stopping him from satisfying the Zukar's demands. And he wanted to kill the interloper there on the spot for it.

"Move it!" Michael gave Faulk a final push. Michael smiled when Faulk's face hit the dirt. "Where's all that training your cuz taught you now?" Michael pulled a struggling Faulk up by his straight black hair. "Humph, I bet you're just too dumb to teach."

Part of him recoiled against taking out his anger on someone else, but he wouldn't deal with the consequences of hesitation because the guilt of being the sole cause of his parents' death was a blow he couldn't live with—he loved them way too much. All he ever wanted to do was make his father proud, and he would, even if it meant killing Daniel and Faulk to do it.

"Leave him alone!" Nickel pleaded, his voice high-pitched, almost like a whine. "We've been able to keep up like you wanted."

"Maybe I wouldn't need to be so rough if he'd tell me where he put my gold egg!" Michael tensed his jaw. If he couldn't get the key from Faulk he wouldn't get the treasure. And if he didn't kill Daniel in the midst of it, he couldn't save his parents. He punched Faulk in the stomach. "Did your cousin tell you how Zukar in training are punished when they fail a job?" He held Faulk by the hair and stared into frightened pupils.

Michael narrowed his eyes at Faulk. He had to get them out of the tunnel soon. If his tracker was correct, they could climb out about a mile further in and they'd be in the blood forest. The border to the prison land. Hopefully, he could cut off Daniel's path and take back what Faulk stole. Having that key would clean up the disaster that Daniel's idiot cousin caused. He landed another blow to Faulk's jaw.

"Stop it!" Nickel cried and fell to his knees. "Please Michael, why are you doing this!"

Michael ignored Nickel, his anger so palatable now he couldn't stop. "Speak, stupid! Tell me where my property is! It's the only reason you're still breathing, idiot." Michael punched Faulk and then backhanded him. This weakling would be the death of them all. "You don't understand what's at risk if you don't give it back!"

Michael released his hair; Faulk fell to the ground. He gave Faulk one final kick in the stomach.

Faulk winced and pressed his lips together. "I don't have it," he groaned. He closed his swollen eye. Faulk swallowed then spit out the mixture of blood.

Michael knew the guy was holding something back from him. But Faulk wouldn't fight back; he just turned away from Michael and struggled to stand.

A moan vibrated through the tunnel. Michael hesitated in his next attack on Faulk, his fist still raised in the air. "Shit, those things are coming our way."

Faulk groaned, and Nickel crawled over to him.

Michael frowned at them. "Get your cousin up and follow me. He better live to give me back what's mine." Leaving them behind was something he wanted to do. If he was honest, he'd like to leave Faulk's cold body behind, but he needed the imbecile as a bargaining tool to get Daniel to be compliant.

Faulk struggled to sit up, glad that Michael was up ahead of them— walking like he had no intention of turning around to help them keep up. "Nickel…can you do me a favor, little dude?"

Nickel sniffed. "I don't know what's happening. Why is Michael acting like this?" He blinked and rubbed his cheek against his shoulder to clear away residue from his tears. "He was nice to me before."

"I don't know what to tell you. He was never nice to me. And I have a problem ticking off people that don't like me." Faulk stood, his muscles twitched and throbbed, but he wouldn't give up. "But I need you to do something. Can you steal his com device from him so I can call Daniel and warn him."

Nickel stepped in front of him. "I can do it. But I need you to loosen these ropes. My father taught Daniel and me how to do it. We have to be back-to-back and do it quick before Michael or the uhum," Nickel tilted his chin at the distant groan of some animal that echoed through the tunnel, "whatever that is finds us."

"Alright, do me first, 'cause I can't do this backwards." Faulk turned around, and within a minute Nickel had loosened the ropes on his wrist.

"Now you can do me."

Faulk hurriedly untied the ropes on Nickel's wrists. "Let's hurry and catch up to him." Faulk walked briskly, even though every step irritated his ribs, and bruises on his chest, he ignored it, determined to end this.

"Where do you think he's taking us?" Nickel asked, jogging alongside Faulk.

"To meet up with Daniel—just what I want him to do. I think Michael's up to something, I just don't know what exactly." Faulk kept a bit of distance from Michael just to have more time to think and figure out what to tell Daniel.

"Why would you think that? Just because you and him argued at everything?" Nickel scratched his head. "Or he could be mad at you because of the card game you won against him."

Faulk snorted. "I might've won all the card games we played, but he didn't want to give up that one treasure, the gold egg he's demanding, when he'd lost and had no other thing to trade."

"So?" Nickel was breathing hard trying to keep pace.

Faulk slowed down a bit. "I don't know. I just got a feeling about it—and the fact that he spent a lot of time studying the map of Uukin, and I sneaked a peek at his notes when he went to the bathroom."

"Oooh, that's bad—but it shows you were at least listening to all that 'instruction' Daniel was giving between the beatings." Nickel laughed.

Faulk raised an eyebrow. "You sure you're only 11 years old, kid? Yeah, I listened, but I looked at Michael's notes—they were all about finding the treasure on Uukin and about some crypt it was kept in. So I didn't buy his story about wanting to change his life like we wanted to."

"What did you think?" Nickel swallowed.

"I don't trust him. He's going to kill us to get to the Warden's wing—at least that's what his notes were about."

"I don't think so. I've known Michael forever, and he's not like that." Nickel shook his head. "If with the plan Daniel came up with, he means it."

"Really, well maybe there's a good reason for it, maybe I'm wrong, but I don't know. Anyhow you and Daniel don't see things from where I'm standing." Faulk slowed down when they caught up to Michael. He put his hands behind his back to feign the appearance that his wrists were still bound.

Nickel gave him a silent wink. Then crept up behind Michael who didn't spare them a glance before he started ranting. "So you finally caught up." Michael hesitated a moment at the growl that vibrated throughout the tunnels. "Good, you're in time for us to climb up." He assessed the jagged holes that littered the side of the uneven wall and lead up to a small hole.

Tripping over his feet, Nickel reached out and snagged Michael's back pocket.

"You stupid kid." Michael smacked Nickel in the chest.

Nickel fell back and whined while kicking the small communicator he lifted out of Michael's pocket to Faulk.

A chomping noise thundered on the wall opposite them. Louder. Louder.

Faulk's hands shook while trying to operate the communicator. "Damnit," he muttered.

Michael lifted Nickel up by his shirt. "What did you do?" His eyes narrowed.

"C'mon," Faulk cursed and flicked the button on the small handheld device. The hairs on his neck stood on edge.

A loud roar boomed behind him, and Faulk dropped the communicator. Michael dropped Nickel.

"Gooooooo!" Michael yelled.

Faulk spared a glance behind him and screamed. A huge wormlike creature, as thick as the tunnel, covered in bonelike spikes was cutting through the dirt a few feet behind them.

Michael quickly scaled the wall.

Faulk sprang to action and surged Nickel forward. His heart thundered in his chest as his hands shook.

"Up! Up...get-up now!" Faulk pushed him and was practically on top of him as they rushed to reach the top before the creature sliced them up against the wall.

"Hurry! It's coming," Nickel cried and reached for Faulk through the hole at the top. His hand beat rapidly on the dirt.

Another growl singed the air around Faulk's feet, and with one final grunt, he pushed himself out of the hole as a bone-colored hook jabbed from the slithering thing beneath him.

"Ah-ha," Faulk's breathing slowed.

Michael hoisted Faulk up by the collar. "Lesson number one, don't-play- with-me!" He punched Faulk out.

Stars. Faulk saw stars in the dark, dingy night, just before his head hit the ground.

16

Daniel placed a hand on Jade's hip. Her stance was rigid but she didn't flinch when he guided her bent wrist. "Picture a dot where you want it to land, and throw—but with enough strength to sink it into the tree."

She nodded. "It feels like…it feels familiar." Jade released the dart at a leaf that was dropping from the tree. The dart sliced through the middle of the leaf to sink deeply into the tree. Her stance relaxed and she laughed.

Bending to get another dart for her, Daniel slid his hand on her arm to grasp her hand lightly. "I'm glad you are remembering to enjoy it." He knew it was a sneaky ploy, but he'd take whatever he could get from her. Being close to her was like drops of water for a thirsty man.

Jade shook her head. "It's more than that. I remember that doing this—throwing things made me feel in control. Like nothing else I did with my family…well, like someone was always deciding for me, telling me I couldn't do something, or that females weren't supposed to do this or that. But when I hold something in my hand, and I decide where it lands, I finally can do something that I want to do." She moved her hand from within his.

"Uhum." Daniel forced back his frown of disappointment. He didn't know how much longer he could slowly get her to fall in love with him again without losing it. His heart already felt ripped with guilt and sadness. Losing his father, now with Faulk and Nickel gone—only made his distance with Jade even harder. Truth was, he wanted to kill something—punch something—yell, scream and dammit even cry. But he wouldn't give in to the weakness, never, because giving in would mean he failed.

"I can do it myself from now on." Jade tossed a hesitant smile over her shoulder at him. Then she refused the dart he held out and picked up the pack on the ground next to them, which was filled with darts.

Daniel stepped back. He'd pushed her far enough, he guessed. "Okay, now aim for different spots on the bark, but this time, make each dart sink deeper than the one before it."

"So, tell me about how we ended up here—in this smelly prison planet." Jade tossed the darts one by one with a precision that demonstrated her returning memory and reflexes.

"Hmm, I'll start at where you tricked me into taking you with me to find my father's killer."

Jade chuckled. "I tricked you," she lifted an eyebrow, "you're that easily manipulated by a girl?"

Daniel smiled easily, feeling a little less on pin-needles while talking to her. "You had a talent for it, since I had a soft spot for you. I'd gone to your house to find a getaway boat. And since Gabe wasn't home, you convince me to take you. But that made it worse since now my cousin Faulk, brother Nickel and I would have to protect you when we knew someone wanted to kill us." There was much more to tell, but Daniel didn't want to focus on the bad part of that journey.

"Then why didn't you leave me somewhere safe? I know my brothers would've found me." Jade tossed another dart. This one landed in the middle of one, pressing the first dart deep within the tree.

"We tried to leave you behind at your family's Trove, but we were afraid the murderers would find you there alone, and that's when you first…" Daniel tilted Jade's chin towards him, "you kissed me." He'd never forget that moment at her family's treasure Trove, another word for a place where every Zukar thief kept their earned riches and built booby traps around their home to protect it.

Shocked registered on her face and her mouth dropped. "I would never have tried to kiss someone. Boys kiss girls—not the other way around." Her eyes dipped to his lips.

"Maybe if I kiss you, you'll remember it?" Daniel smirked. Oh, he knew this was the worst kind of manipulation, but Jade hardly ever turned down a challenge.

Jade's eyes blinked. She swallowed. "Maybe," she whispered.

Daniel leaned in—not giving her time to change her mind—and gently touched his lips to hers. The familiar zing, and softness of her full lips made him groan. Jade's bottom lip trembled, and Daniel couldn't help but deepen the kiss as she released a gasp.

Jade relaxed. Then slid her arms around Daniel's neck as she snuggled closer. Reluctantly, she gently pushed him away. "Uh-uh. I don't remember kissing you."

Daniel cleared his throat. "Do you remember kissing anyone?"

Her arms unraveled from Daniel's neck and she shrugged away from him. "Yes." She frowned slightly. "He was tall, like you, had slanted, exotic dark eyes, a dimple and straight black hair."

"Faulk," Daniel muttered, his fists balled up. She'd remembered his cousin—but not him. He raked a hand through his hair. "You didn't kiss him. Tell me what you remember."

Jade tossed a dart over her shoulder as her eyes traveled down Daniel's face to his chest. "Let me think." Her eyebrows lifted. "We were on a boat, and I was handing him a sandwich."

"And…" Daniel would choke Faulk if he found out he'd kissed Jade and didn't tell him.

"That's when he gave me a quick kiss on the lips." Jade tapped her lip with her forefinger. "But it could've been a dream. It's still foggy."

Daniel gulped down the irritation he felt at this new information Jade was sharing with him. Neither she nor Faulk had told him they'd kissed before. He hoped that maybe her memory was still jumbled. "How does it make you feel—remembering his kiss?"

"I don't know. I feel nothing about it." Her head tilted to the side and she pivoted around to toss a few darts that seemed to roll out of her fingers. "I just remember it happening."

"Oh, well ah…" Daniel was at a loss for words, his heart squeezed in his chest at the thought that she'd even considered being with someone besides him. He knew he was her first kiss, so if she had kissed Faulk it must've happened afterward.

"What else happened on our adventure?" Jade's tone seemed relaxed, friendly, like she was teasing him.

He placed his hands on his hips to stop himself from snagging her back into his arms and ignoring the mistakes he'd made by bringing her here. But instead, he cleared his throat. "We escaped the killer, but ended up setting off the treasure my father had hidden. It was like a time bomb, and was destroying Merwin by decaying it from the inside out. We went to the origin of the treasure—called a pakeet to stop it."

"Your father? Was his name Rayne? I remember him. He used to give me sweet blooms to eat when he came over to talk to my dad." Jade tested the point of a dart on the tip of her finger then pivoted around to throw it over her shoulder.

"Yeah, him and Bry were like brothers. He knew you loved the sweet blooms."

A frown marred her brow. "Who killed him? Was it someone from the other Zukar guilds?"

Daniel knew many of the kids whose parents worked the other guilds in the Zukar clans. Each group specialized in something different, but all of it surrounded treasure hunting or paid jobs. "No, it was his and your father's best friend—Haden."

Jade dropped the bag with the darts in them. Her hands rubbed her arms, and she shivered. "Haden? H-he was like family to us. How could he? Why…"

"Because he wanted the pakeet. It had the power to rebuild or destroy worlds. He died trying to kill us for it."

"Did we save Merwin? Destroy the pakeet?" Jade appeared enthralled, as though Daniel was telling her a made up story.

Daniel hugged her close, and she trembled. "We proved ourselves to the alien race who created the device and we carry the pakeet within all of us—me, you, Faulk, and Nickel—can use it together when we are of like mind and purpose, to save worlds."

Jade sniffed. "We did that? I helped?"

"You did, and we did—together." He smiled at her, proud of her part in the outcome of the adventure. "I couldn't have succeeded without you."

17

Daniel leaned back on the bark of the tree while repacking his backpack.

Gabe sat next to him. "I'm scared as shit to take her out there." He twisted the end of one of his beaded brown braids between his finger and thumb.

"Me too." Daniel frowned at his communicator and read the cryptic message sent from Michael's com device, *Danger with M. – Faulk.* His lips thinned in surprise that the com was working considering Michael had cut them off from contact earlier. He grunted, not knowing what to make of the message. But knowing it spurned fire under his nagging suspicions concerning Michael.

"Does she seem okay to you?" Gabe asked with a hitch in his voice.

Daniel knew that tone. It was Gabe's freaked out one. "Why do you ask that? She lost her memory, almost died —again—because of me, and came back to us. She's a freakin' miracle right now."

"Yeah, I get that—but she's *different*." Gabe tilted forward to rest his elbows on his knees.

"What's she doing now?" Daniel stuffed the communicator in the small pocket on his leather belt.

"Well—let me recollect…she was tossing darts, then did it faster, faster then faster. Um, then she asked me to toss knives at her." He cleared his throat.

"Knives?" Daniel's eyebrow lifted. That was strange, Jade at times practiced speed, but never with them throwing objects at her at the same time—he wondered where or why she'd asked Gabe to do it.

"Yeah." He swallowed. "And she uh…"

"Did you? Did you throw knives at your baby sister?" Daniel knew the answer. It would be no, since Gabe would never do anything he thought would hurt Jade. All of them wanted to protect her or teach her to take care of herself but not put her in the position to take any risk.

"At first I didn't—but then, man, she looked at me—angry—like I've never seen her, and she said real low, 'some brother you are, if you were half the brother you say you were, you'd want me to protect myself—now throw the damn knife!' Just like that, she said it."

"Damn," Daniel knew then that Gabe was right, Jade had never been that aggressive with any of them. Whiny—she did that, but demanding and harsh—never. "What happened then?" Daniel didn't know if he really wanted to know, but he had to. The damage was something he'd caused inadvertently by bringing her, and he had to know if it was something he could fix.

"I did it, but didn't toss them at her but near her." Gabe wiped his hands down his face, clasping them over his eyes and nose like he was collecting his composure. "And she yelled at me, 'Attack me dammit!' so I did, and she caught it—like it was nothing. Caught every knife I threw and then she tossed the damned things into the tree like a madwoman."

"God…what did we do?" Daniel's hand was shaking.

"I don't know. It's like she has no fear. None, like she's forgotten every single boundary, caution, or warning we've given her." Gabe crossed his arms to rest on his knees. "It's not that I don't know she will be able to handle herself with the guards—it's that she's unstable. I don't know her, not like she was before, my sister just seems to be as much of a fighter as me or my brothers now. And I don't know...I just don't know."

"Maybe that's it, maybe she just lost her fear—something we have constantly reminded her of every day since we thought that as a girl she was weaker." Daniel bit his lower lip. He hoped the explanation he gave was the truth, because if they were going to make it off this planet alive, he needed Jade to be as fierce as he'd known she could be, but never had the opportunity to prove like he had.

"I hope that's all it is because I can't take her back to my parents this way." Gabe stood up. "After the way I left her behind when I went to see my girlfriend before everything went to crap and we had to run. Then she went with you. I've screwed up, over and over again as the man my father wanted me to be. The protector for Jade. It's to the point where I don't think I'll ever be able to look my dad in the eye again."

Daniel sprung up beside him. "It's not your fault. I'm the one who took her with me—I shouldn't have but I did. Bry trusted me to. And I knew better than to put her in danger—not once, but three times. There's a use for the pakeet in her. The alien race that entrusted us with it, did it for a good reason. We just don't know what reason that is yet. Our parents saw the pakeet as a blessing and a curse. For that reason, we all must stick together to protect it."

Gabe waved. "It doesn't matter. We're here now. We need to finish this."

"Yeah, and what does that mean to you, Gabe?" Daniel lifted his eyebrow. "To me that means when we get Michael, Faulk and Nickel, we leave here."

Gabe nodded. "You're right, I'm done with this. But what about you wanting to change? You know, save people who were enslaved here like the King of Merwin would've done to you and your brother. The King of Merwin who wanted to send you to this planet. Don't you want some revenge in that? Isn't it really revenge you are seeking and not this transformation from thief to good guy you are portraying you want to be?"

"I still want to become the good guy. If I was honest, I want the revenge in it too. But getting Jade off this planet and out of danger is more important to me now. Maybe…hell, I don't know, maybe changing my life just means putting someone else before myself – before what I want. I'd trusted the Sira Zukar. And serving the king of thieves had been my dream then. Now we can trust no one." Daniel growled. "I was stupid!" He punched the tree. "I am stupid—to think I could figure this out without my father."

"Hey." Gabe slapped Daniel's back. "Our father's made mistakes like we are gonna, and they figured it out, right?"

Daniel jerked Gabe's hand off his shoulder. "Did they? Hard to freakin' tell with my father dead and yours probably on the run for his life right now."

"So what do we do—go back to Merwin with a failed mission?" Gabe shrugged. "Because that's what my father would remind me of— 'Zukars never back out of a job,' and isn't that what we would be doing." Gabe's shoulders slouched. "But I'd do it in a minute if that meant saving Jade."

"Me too. Me too." Daniel nodded. "And that's got to be what we do, get the others and leave!"

Gabe sighed. "We good?"

"Yeah. But we need to straighten out this thing with Michael and Faulk. He's my cousin, and I have to take care of him. Even if that means kicking Michael's ass myself." He lifted an eyebrow. "Got that? Will you stay out of it?"

Gabe shrugged. "If you want, but you know Michael's a dirty fighter. And you, my friend, may need my help remember?"

"Not. Besides, getting the treasure from the Warden would've been a death wish." Daniel shrugged, refusing to admit to himself that part of him, the taunting part of him down deep, felt a rush, a thrill at the possibility of plucking the trinket from the evil bastard. But he tamped that feeling down. Saving Jade was more important.

"We could've done it. It would've been worth it. Legend said the owner has the ability to manipulate the minds of men." Gabe grinned, that hungry look of greed glowed in the depths of his eyes.

"But with everything, there's a price. No one knows what price using that treasure includes. With the pakeet, all of us had to risk our lives—almost to our deaths, and through so much pain we'd wished we were dead. I bet the treasure the Warden holds costs even more."

Footsteps sounded behind them. "Talking about another treasure, boys?"

Daniel pivoted around to smile at Jade. "No—just a legend."

Her eyebrow lifted. "Does your father have a trove on Merwin like mine?"

"Bigger. A place of fire and gold…an island of riches he'd collected his entire life. Do you remember going there with me?"

She frowned and rolled a dart between her fingers. "No. But I remember my father's trove. Sands of green, gold and black littered the beaches. Trees, weeping willows that loved to eat people, and sea monsters that protected the entrances. Did yours have that?"

He grinned. "More: boiling sea waters, transparent fish filled with fire, a metallic-colored serpent that swam in our own river of molten gold."

"Daniel's father, Rayne, had the most coveted treasure trove of all Zukars. His was un-touchable for thousands of years. No one ever could figure out how Rayne was able to claim it."

"Wow…I wish I could remember it." Her gaze slipped from Daniel's eyes to his lips. A hungry expression bloomed, then was suppressed as she blinked.

Gabe cleared his throat. "We need to get moving. Franz had a window in the security break to send me a message. He said the only way we can run into Michael is where the tunnels and the forest meet."

Daniel dragged his eyes from Jade's playful flirt. "Where?"

"There's like a border leading to the prison that's not as protected as the main area. The Tar lands," Gabe stated, gruffly.

Jade went over to pick up her pack. "I don't think I like the sound of it."

"Me neither." Daniel grabbed up his gear. "But we go." The message sent from Michael's com had him wondering just what Michael had planned for them, but a smirk slid on Daniel's face at the fact that he had something waiting for Michael as well.

18

"This place stinks." Daniel grimaced and squeezed his nose. "You sure this is just tar?"

The expanse in front of them was a river of a dark, thick substance that snaked between protruding smooth black rocks. It bubbled, it smelled, and Daniel would bet—something lived in it. Beyond it was a border of thick bushes that formed a barrier of gold trimmed leaves. The border almost appeared beautiful compared to the rest of the planet he'd seen so far—except for the fact that once they breached those firmly packed leaves, guardians of the jail could be—probably would be—waiting for them.

"The whole planet reeks like rotten flesh. I'm used to it." Gabe nudged him with his elbow and peeked over his shoulder at Jade.

"I agree, but I don't think I'll get used to it." Jade tightened the strap on her pack. Then she ran her fingers over the darts on her belt which created the nasty sometimes poisonous weapons as needed. "Do you think those rocks are safe to jump on?" Her back straightened. Jade narrowed her gaze on several of the rock platforms as if measuring them for their safety.

"I got something we can use to check." Daniel tossed a small flat device onto one of them. He twisted his wrist and tapped the thin band. A 3-D image sprang up with the depth and dimension of the rock platform within the dense murky sludge in front of them. "It's safe, but only one of us can fit on one at a time."

"Got that, so you go first." Gabe stepped closer to Daniel and placed his palm over the image. It collapsed.

Jade hummed, something she did when she was contemplating something. "I know. You want me to go in the middle, right?" Jade smirked.

Daniel's eyebrow lifted. That was something the old Jade would say. Maybe, what Gabe feared wasn't true. Jade wasn't taking any unnecessary risks like they'd feared. "Yeah, it's best since we don't know what could be waiting for us once we clear this," he waved a hand in front of him, "tar or whatever."

"I would be able to handle anything thrown our way, you know?" Jade lifted her eyebrow in return with a teasing mimic. "Since I'm lighter than you both, if I went first I wouldn't be as likely to jar any of the rocks and make it more difficult for you both to follow me." Her chin went upward in a silent dare for him to respond.

"That so? But seeing as though I'm the one calling the shots on this, I need you to cooperate with us." Daniel moved close to her, his heart clenched with a sharp pain from the guilt of possibly endangering her again. "Please, this time, just do what I ask." He caressed her cheek. "I love you and I can't survive another near-death experience with you, now—or ever. You might not realize it yet, but you mean more to me than anyone, and I just need you to let me take the lead on this." He leaned closer, "Can you?"

Jade blinked back the moisture that gathered in her eyes and nodded back at him. Then she laid her hand on his. "For my friend, I can do it."

"Friend?" Daniel gave her a wry smile. "If that's all you can afford to give me of your heart right now, I'll take it." He dropped his hand and pointed to Gabe. "The rear, and if you see me get into any trouble when I get on the other side, lead her back from where we came."

"Definitely." Gabe slapped hands with Daniel then stepped back next to Jade.

Daniel didn't bother to ponder the danger of jumping near the apparently boiling molten liquid. He landed on the firm gray rock, which was wider than the expanse of his arms he held outward while balancing. His chest throbbed. He took a deep breath. Then leaped to the next rock. Daniel didn't allow himself to look back at Jade's progress, he trusted Gabe to take care of her. He just wanted this over with. The next one was closer.

His gaze caught a flash of something metallic, and a slight muted splash was coming toward the next rock. Daniel held up his hand, signaling for the others to stop. Then his eyes landed on Jade's.

She stood perfectly still, her hand raised, dart aimed as her eyes followed the silvery serpent whose tail was sinking within the lake of tar. Her finger rested in front of her lips and she mouthed, "It's gone."

Daniel gave her a thumbs-up. He twisted around and repeated the signal to Gabe. Blood pounded through his veins, so strong he could feel it. This was it. The rush he'd lived for. What drove him and tempted him to be a Zukar—the thrill. Where he'd get that from now, he didn't know. This new road to changing his life was turning out to be a failure. He landed on the rock with ease. Just two more to go. But his troubled thoughts wouldn't leave him alone. When they left this planet, he'd go home—to the only home he'd ever known: Merwin. And the King wouldn't have a prison planet left to send him to. At least then he could try to figure out what kind of life he could lead on a planet full of thieves and cut-throats he'd once been a part of. His father had considered running as an answer. Maybe it wasn't. Maybe he could do something greater.

Daniel made the final jump. He peered over his shoulder at Jade who was to the side of him. Daniel released a sigh of relief, then pulled out his gun and waited for her.

Jade landed beside Daniel, who steadied her. "Something's coming!"

Daniel's gaze jerked to Gabe. "Damn!" A roar rent through the air.

Gabe stumbled while landing two rocks from the border where Daniel and Jade stood.

"Hurry up!" Daniel called. His hands flexing, ready for a fight. Losing Gabe wasn't a possibility. He'd kill the beast with his bare hands—fighting till the end was what a Zukar was made for.

"Tryin'!" Gabe jumped. One rock left between him and the others. Fear was etched on his tight features.

"Faster dammit!" Daniel waved him on.

Gabe hesitated, then jumped just as the silver tail of the serpent whipped up and slapped his leg. It burned a hole through his pants and sliced his skin. "Arrrrrgh!" He dived forward and slid several feet onto the pebbled black ground. "Hurts!" Gabe's leg bent up and he grasped his knee with both hands, rolling side to side.

Daniel rushed to him and crouched beside him. "Hold still." He swallowed and hesitantly touched the wound. The tail had burned a deep gash into Gabe's calf, to the bone, it appeared. Material from his pants had seared into the skin. The wound was open and bleeding.

"It's bad, man."

"Shit. Walking on this is going to be hell." Gabe growled.

Jade sat next to him. "Do you have something to take away his pain—so we can get him somewhere safe?"

Daniel shrugged off his backpack, reached inside and pulled out a syringe with multi-colored purple and gold flecks of medicine within. "This will hold him—for a while. It won't heal it completely though. Put something hard in his mouth. This is going to hurt."

Jade slid off one of the leather straps on her belt. She placed it between Gabe's lips. "His eyes looked glazed over."

"He's in shock. This will help." Daniel squeezed Gabe's foot between his legs then poised the syringe on the side of his calf. "Ready?"

Jade nodded.

Daniel slowly pressed the medicine into Gabe's wound.

The area swelled, turning a dark green hue. Within seconds, he seemed to absorb the liquid. Gabe convulsed, his head jerked and Jade fought to keep the leather strap between his lips. Suddenly, as if a switch turned off, Gabe's body relaxed. His breathing went to normal and the bleeding slowed.

"Gabe?" Jade smacked his face gently.

"Yeah?" Gabe opened his eyes. "My stomach hurts. And the leg still hurts, but the edge is off and I can move."

"Good, because given all the crying like a baby you just did, I'm sure the guards are alerted we're here." Daniel tried to make light of the situation as he helped Gabe up.

"I wasn't crying, I was cursing." Gabe balanced on one leg, allowing the front of his foot to keep him steady. His hand squeezed a piece of Daniel's vest.

"We have to move. Are you really ready?" Daniel asked.

"Have to be, I want to live, right?" Gabe chuckled brokenly.

Jade slid an arm up under Gabe's. "Yes, you have to take care of me, right?"

"I wonder," Gabe answered.

19

Daniel didn't feel good about this at all. Gabe could barely walk. With him like this and Jade possibly unstable, no way they'd be able to fight off a guard attack. Damn. He braced Gabe more tightly with his arm, trying to take some of the weight off Gabe's good leg.

"You doing alright?" Daniel asked and observed Gabe's reaction. The dense land scattered with bushes that stood over Daniel's 6ft frame gave them little room to maneuver.

"Hangin' in I guess. Sorry about this," Gabe grunted.

"It's not your fault, it's mine. I brought us here knowing this place was rough and it was a crazy idea to think we'd be able to even find our way to the jail. Although Franz's blueprint looked wicked enough to make any Zukar's mouth water at the challenge."

Gabe chuckled. "I know. It was slick the way he got it using the Warden's own security system's signals to locate the walls and crevices. Franz has a talent the Zukar praised him for. They said he was even better at tactical planning than my father. We were lucky to have him come with us and be our eyes and ears."

Jade shifted Gabe's arm over her shoulder. "You think he'll be mad that we are turning back since he did so much work to prepare?"

"Hell yeah, but he'll get over it. He's different from Michael—he doesn't stay angry long." Gabe hopped on one foot over a twisted vine embedded in the ground.

"You're right about that, Michael can stew on something forever. I think he has a permanent pissed off frown on his face." Daniel's arm brushed against another tree. A noise, faint but close, tickled his ear. "Shh."

He came to an abrupt stop. Just what they needed, damn guards, he signaled to Jade to keep up with him. Spotting a burrow just under a nearby bush, he pointed to it and practically dragged Gabe with him.

"We all can't fit in there," Gabe whispered and struggled against Daniel.

"You're going in. I'll stand lead with Jade between us." Daniel yanked Gabe with him and tried to push him into the hole, the rustle of bushes was getting closer. Inhuman grunts and yelps sounded in front of them.

"No! You protect Jade, with this bum leg I'll get myself captured, eventually. At least they'll give me some medical care if they want me to work." Gabe pushed Daniel's chest.

"Gabe, don't!" Jade pleaded in a broken whisper. "Please don't leave us."

"I'm not, I'm going to detour, but Daniel will save me, get me out with the other prisoners." Gabe pushed at Jade who fell back into the trunk of the bush.

"Why do this? You know I'd die protecting you—" Daniel stepped to him.

"And get us all killed. Trust me, you both hide in there and I'll divert them. I have an implant Franz had me swallow—you do too, remember? You'll be able to find me."

Daniel blinked back his fear; he had no choice. "Fine, I'll save your ass."

"You too! And you better come get me," Gabe hobbled off, calling over his shoulder, "and protect her for me."

Jade stood behind him with a shocked and tormented expression while she silently cried, her hands fisted at her sides before she rubbed her arms. "What now?"

"Get inside, and I'll squeeze in next to you. Maybe if we wait long enough, Michael and the others will show up. Now go!" Daniel pushed her down through the depths of the hole and squeezed in snugly beside her. He used his hand to pull some loose branches in place. Gunshots. Screaming. Yelling. Jade jumped in his arms and buried her face in his neck.

Gabe's voice sounded in distant admission, "I'm alone I'm telling you! I got discharged by the Merwin guard."

Daniel shut his eyes against the most tortured scream he'd ever heard leave Gabe's lips, and wrapped his arm around a sobbing Jade. Daniel swallowed his own pain, Gabe had said he would give a signal that all was well—but Daniel knew, the scream from Gabe's lips wasn't the warning intended.

M ichael couldn't stand to look at them. This final tunnel would be the last before he met up with Daniel. And Faulk better be telling the truth or he'd kill him dead on the spot for nearly ruining everything. He'd never be able to figure out why Daniel didn't send his weak, dumb-ass cousin back to Earth where he'd come from. Michael was fighting against everything in him not to literally lose it.

"Move it!" Michael gritted his teeth and pushed Faulk forward. He spied Nickel who was quietly jogging alongside them. "And you, do you know where your cousin put my gold egg?"

"No, I didn't know he stole nothin' from you." Nickel didn't turn towards Michael but kept his eyes to the ground.

"You'll be the one to get it from Daniel. If you do, I won't kill him—this time. I can't make the same promise for your cousin here," Michael spat.

"Why do you want to kill him? Your father said you were our family, and if I'm your family then so is Faulk because he's my cousin," Nickel stated quietly.

"I never considered you or Daniel my cousins. You're not my blood, and I got enough brothers. Daniel and Gabe are just friends and that doesn't run deep like what my brothers and I have."

"But—" Nickel's rejected plea was cut off.

"I never even liked Daniel and never pretended I did so why would you think I'd consider him anything to me?" He kicked Faulk's lower back. "Climb up and out of here first. Look out for guards and be quiet. I'd gladly sacrifice your life for Nickel's since he can get what I want from Daniel."

Faulk cleared his throat. "I don't think so. Not even Nickel knows where it is, and I'm not talking unless I lay my eyes on Daniel and make sure Nickel is safe." His back straightened as though he was challenging Michael.

"Uh-hum, I think you're lying to me about something." Michael jerked Faulk around, nose-to-nose. He gritted his teeth and asked, "Are you?"

Faulk's eyes widened slightly, but his muscles tightened against Michael's tugging. "Are you the real liar here, Michael? It doesn't seem like you are telling us the truth about why the stupid egg is so important. Important enough to kill me, ruin the bond you have with Daniel, and to turn your back on your father's direction to keep us safe and treat us like your own blood."

Michael released Faulk, his tongue filled with the bitterness of distaste. A tinge of guilt teased his chest, but he punched Faulk in the face anyway. "Shut up! I decide what's best. And if I don't get what's mine from you, then one of you will pay the price. That's it. I'm going to take special pleasure in making sure it's you."

Faulk shook his head against the blinding blow. Then he blinked, and pushed his shoulders back. "If you are sending me up first, are you saying you trust me to be the lookout?"

"I'm saying you *will* be the lookout if you want Nickel safe. But if you both want to be safe, you'll shut your mouth and cooperate. We need to find Daniel. After I get what I want from him, we'll be good." Michael didn't flinch at the delivery of that lie. If he was going to fulfill the request made by the Sira Zukar, he'd have to bring back the treasure and proof of Daniel's death. That was something that would bring him some pleasure. Michael's hate of Daniel simmered from the moment Michael's father insisted on comparing their accomplishments as recruits to the Zukar. Given the fact that his own father was in danger because of Daniel only made his disdain grow, and he needed it to, because failure wasn't an option.

"Why? What…did I do to you to make you hate me?" Faulk asked, with a bit of steel in his voice.

"You came here. Now shut your mouth and get up there. Warn us if you hear anything."

Faulk gingerly climbed the side of the tunnel, and the stench of the heated air from it was left behind. Once he cleared the top he called down to them with a loud whisper, "It's clear."

Michael frowned at Nickel. "I go and then you follow. If you hear anything then stay down here." Even though he didn't have any love for the kid, he didn't want him to suffer what the guards did to children of the Zukar. If Faulk was captured, then he'd be able to get away, but Nickel would only slow him down. The kid would be safer left behind. Without a backward glance, he warned, "Don't stay down here too long after I get moving there—or you'll be left behind."

"I won't." Nickel shuffled his feet and waited until Michael's head cleared the opening before he started to climb.

Michael swallowed against the putrid smell of burning tar that filled the air, and twisted around to glance at the boiling lake. Straight ahead, thick bushes led to where he knew he'd find Daniel. He adjusted the tracker he'd set on his wrist to keep following Daniel.

Unfortunately, it only worked in intermittent cycles since it concealed itself from the scanning of the security monitoring on the planet. He tilted his chin toward the dark skies and grinned, knowing Franz's talent hid them well from the guards.

"Stay behind me. Once we get in there, I'm not stopping until I find Daniel." His lip turned up, his eyes narrowed, and he resolved himself to the fact that if all went well someone would die today.

21

Daniel slid his arm from around Jade's waist. "We should crawl out of here," he whispered. Making sure the area was clear, he squeezed out of the hole. He checked the tracking device on his wrist and noted that the security sensors would rotate around in another hour or so. They were clear for a sliver of time.

"Are we going to save him now?" Jade pushed herself out of the hole and placed her foot on one of the thick roots of the bush to hop up. She dug in the pouch on her belt for a dart and rolled it between her fingers. "These have explosives in them." Jade grinned, reminding Daniel of her mischievous nature before her recent memory loss.

Daniel's eyebrow lifted. "Where did you get those?"

"I made them from the powder Gabe keeps in his pouch. You guys were talking and I lifted it out of his bag. Since we were going to be running into guards I thought I should make something that could stop more than one of them at a time." She smiled wryly at him. "I didn't think I'd have to use them to save my brother though."

That comment sliced Daniel's chest like a knife. Jade's father had to kill Haden, Bry's once best friend. Hopefully, revenge from the

Zukar wasn't in place due to the loss of the traitor to both Daniel's father and the Sira Zukar. Was that how it would be for them? He hoped not, he didn't want to cause the death of Jade or anyone in her family. Maybe after this he'd let her go. It would rip his heart out to do it, make the treasure they found together useless, but if it made her happy, he'd risk it. "Me neither. But he did it to save you." Something Daniel admitted to himself, he kept failing to do.

"Maybe so, but he wanted to save you too." Her eyelids dipped and she turned away to mumble, "I'd want you saved."

Daniel smiled at that, but it didn't fill him with as much joy as it would've a month ago. Now he felt isolated, alone and like a failure. Nothing he'd planned had worked out. Catching up with Michael to save Faulk and Nickel wouldn't conclude his trip here at Uukin because there was no way in hell he would leave without his best friend. Even if that meant he died trying.

"It won't be long, I don't think." Daniel frowned against the image of Michael that sprang up in his mind. He knew Michael would take this small window of opportunity to close in on them.

"For what?" Jade's expression hardened. "We have to hurry and go after Gabe. His scream—it didn't sound well at all."

"I know, but not without Michael and the others. Gabe wanted us to wait for them. And we will. But I know Michael will take the hint from your brother, Franz's warning signal countdown. The guards seemed to have pulled back after they took Gabe. Franz was able to shield us from them so they bailed—for now." His hand tensed on his gun.

"I-I miss him. You know he told me stories at night when I had trouble sleeping?" She crossed her arms. "Even Michael teased him about it."

Daniel gave her a lopsided grin. "I can see that." He moved closer and enveloped her in his arms. "We'll get him back." He snuck a kiss to her cheek. Jade shivered like she used to whenever he touched her. A nervous excitement that thrilled him each time he held her before he realized a change in her.

"Will we? Or are we going to die in there?" Her eyes watered.

"Hey, trust me on this—I'd die saving him. Gabe and our friendship go beyond being thrown together. I will not leave here without him." Hesitantly, Daniel leaned down to touch his lips to hers, begging with his heart that she wouldn't push him away. He hoped this wasn't the last kiss they'd share, but the chances were great that it could be. He couldn't stop the slight tremble of his hand that rested on her hip when she kissed him back.

Jade deepened the kiss, then pulled away slightly to land a small peck to his lips as if she couldn't help herself. "I wish...so wish I could remember when we were in love. Because...I feel..."

Daniel heard a small squeaking sound, and placed his finger to her full lips to silence her. "Shhh." Part of him wanted to stay in that place where Jade's kiss put him, a place of hope. But the muffled sound he heard meant more guards or—Michael. He stepped around her, crouched low and pulled out his knife. His mouth watered at the possibilities of kicking Michael's butt; his eyes traveled through the thick, tall bushes covered in black leaves trimmed in gold.

There. Sneaking through two closely tangled bushes he saw Michael squeezing through. Daniel lunged. Dropped his knife. Landed a punch to the side of Michael's dimpled chin.

Michael kicked out, knocking Daniel to the ground. "You want this?" He hit his chest and steadied himself.

"You!" Daniel pounded upwards into Michael's face. One punch after another, his chest thundered. Anger flared. His teeth clenched against returning blows.

Michael kneed him in the stomach. Then squatted and pulled his booted foot back for a swift kick. Where Daniel showed anger, Michael responded with a detached coolness and methodical technique born of a trained killer.

"Stop!" Faulk tried to pull Michael off Daniel. But Michael wouldn't budge.

"Michael!" Jade yelled. "Don't do this. Gabe's captured." She stepped forward to stand just in front of where Daniel's head hit on the ground.

Whipping his head back, Michael busted Faulk in the nose with his head and jabbed Daniel's face again, releasing a growl.

Daniel twisted and unseated Michael then scrambled on top of him to land a blow. "Listen to her!" He spit blood from his mouth and grabbed Michael by the neck.

Michael pulled his gun from his hip, and pointed it at Daniel's chin. "I heard her. Gabe got captured—because of you. Give me one reason why I shouldn't shoot you now."

Jade fell on her knees at Michael's feet. "Don't do this. We have to save him."

Daniel narrowed his gaze and adrenaline simmered deep in his chest. "You need me to save him. I know where they took him."

A light danced on the tip of Michael's gun. "You better or—"

"Drop it, Michael!" Jade yelled. "Don't do this. We have to work together." Jade's face turned rigid. "I mean it, or it'll be four against one and we'll go save Gabe without you!"

The hairs on Daniel's neck rose, and the last thought he had before he threw his knife at the dark figure beyond the bush was, *I'm not dying today.*

Daniel braced himself as several thick figures burst through the black bush.

The prison guards muscled arms pumped as they charged.

The things would almost look humanoid if it wasn't for the fact that their skin was layered with thick ropes of flesh that resembled tangles of burnt and twisted skin. Their mouths were overcrowded with jagged pointed teeth. Pulled chunky meat hung over their multitude of beady eyes. Tiny ears were holes tucked under a small slab of skin. Their fingers were tipped with extendable claws that appeared to grow and throb with each step. And chains of metal covered parts of their bulging chest and legs.

Jade stilled beside Daniel as he rose. "Get behind me." He flicked his gun from his waist and fired at them.

Michael flipped over and shot several of them in the eyes. Behind him, Jade tossed dart upon dart with deadly precision that exploded within the eye tissue of many bringing them down.

"Run!" Faulk yelled and grabbed Nickel by the arm, pushing the kid behind him.

"There's nowhere…" Jade grabbed more darts from her belt.

Nets spewed from the palms of several of the guards, slamming Daniel backwards and pinning him to the ground. Daniel fell. Pain, burning, and electrical shocks ravaged his body. He screamed. Belief that something so painful could be expelled from the bodies of these beasts made him think that maybe breaking into the jail wasn't a good idea after all.

"Don't fight!" Daniel said through trembling lips. He prayed that the others wouldn't suffer, but squeezed his eyes shut against the threatening of tears caused the echoing cries of those around him. The more he fought the ropes, the more searing pain thundered through his body. At that moment, he knew what had caused Gabe's scream.

22

Daniel was reduced to growling. His gaze followed the guard as he removed the stakes from the net. They were metal, thick and topped with a never ending flame it seemed. The burning from the unforgiving ropes was giving off a mild electrical charge that caused Daniel's body to twitch uncontrollably. But at least now Daniel was used to it. He forced his mind to focus on something else, on taking down the next guard, on holding things together till a break presented itself and he could get away.

The guard removed the last stake from the ground. Its multiple eyes squinting as it warned, "You move – I slice off your foot."

Daniel bit down on his tongue to hold his anger in check. *Think. Think. Think.* His movement stilled at hearing Jade cry out.

The guard made popping sounds expelled from slivers in its skin and signaled to the other one standing over Nickel, who was shivering uncontrollably. "Release them. We make them walk on their own. If they run – maim them. The doctors will heal them for work later."

Daniel forced himself to remain still while the other guard snarled in return.

"You? The leader of them," one of the tallest guards asked, its thick-clawed finger jabbing at Daniel though the net.

"Yeah." Daniel's mouth was dry, his skin still throbbing. But he didn't move.

"Tell them to do as I say and to follow you." The guard retracted the net back within its palm. Then it signaled to Daniel to stand. "Get up. This is the beginning of your service," he laughed.

Standing up on wobbling legs, Daniel forced his muscles to lock against the aches. He waited while Nickel stumbled over to him. Daniel reached back to steady him.

"No touching!" another guard called from behind them.

Daniel nodded to Nickel, and clasped his hand over the small weapon Nickel slipped him. He could always count on his brother to use his size and apparent innocence to their benefit. Their father did his job teaching them the mechanics of how to survive, but Daniel wished he would've listened more. The barren land of Uukin, and the thick, spotted fair skin of the monstrous guards reminded Daniel of the void he felt inside. The regret of possible failure taunted him, but he straightened his shoulders and winked back at his brother. He had to do this for Nickel, for Jade and Faulk. To save, Gabe he'd give his life as his friend had for them. Whether he and Michael could work out their mutual dislike for each other or not, he would do right by Gabe.

"Move faster!" the guard next to Daniel threatened, his large hand appeared like it was bandaged by burnt and twisted skin. Thick bent fingers sprouted out of the warped flesh and yellowed, curved nails poked from the middle.

His steps quickened, and Daniel snuck a glance behind him at the others who stayed closely in line. Nickel practically jogged to keep up as they walked through a narrow path within the bushes which the guards seemed to know without fault. Nickel's grimace gave away the slow recovery from the sting of the nets.

The jagged edges of the gold trimmed leaves scratched against his face. As they continued on, the metallic smell of the planet grew more pungent but was mixed with the sour odor of rotting flesh.

"Walk and spit," a guard demanded.

Faulk coughed again, and the constant rush of vomit splashed against the firm packed dirt. "I can't stop." Another gush poured out of Faulk's mouth.

The guard behind Daniel made a few popping sounds and the one ahead stopped abruptly.

"This one's sick," the beast next to Faulk told another, who went to investigate.

"I'll be okay," Faulk replied hoarsely and stumbled into the guard next to him.

"Hurry up and get better, we leave now!" the guards guttural smacks and hand waving got a responding nod from the guard ahead and they started walking again. Then he pulled Faulk up by his collar. He searched for Daniel and stumbled closer to the others.

Daniel was the first of them to clear the thick bush to the flat and smooth rock terrain. The guard beside him belted out a series of pops and growls. The ground shook, and within seconds, speared rocks popped out rocky surface. More rumbling and masses of huge mushroomed tipped metal structures, hundreds of them, rose from the ground. Daniel braced himself. This was it. He couldn't lie to himself, he was pumped with the challenge of breaking everyone out of this place—at least the innocent ones.

"Move," someone commanded.

Daniel made sure Faulk had recovered from his sickness and he pushed on. He stepped around the scattering of spiked rocks that littered their path. Steam rose from the tops of the structures and

Daniel wondered at how the guards would get them inside. Then one of the guards pulled out a cylinder shaped handheld device. As Daniel walked forward, the guard pressed the tip of the spear shaped cylinder to the side of the base of the structure that stood over 80 feet high. The sky was clear, and stars sparkled in the night. Daniel thought it was beautiful, with the exception of the minefield of stove-piped mushrooms that extended from the ground. Thundering clicking sounds continued, and plates within the dirt moved to pushed up additional structures that connected the rounded features together. The buildings groaned and popped as they slid into place, creating multiple levels of doomed dark metal areas that were connected by enclosed piped tunnels.

Daniel frowned. This wasn't what he expected. From his research on the place, it was underground. Shit. If the records the Zukar kept were inaccurate, saving Gabe might turn into a disaster. He couldn't – hell, wouldn't—let that happen. He'd kill the Warden first with his bare hands before he failed. One thing being a trained Zukar prepared him for was – surprises. His father made sure to remind him to expect the unexpected. And now he admitted he liked it that way. Every cell in his body came alive. This was it – what the depths of his being had been waiting for, a challenge.

His thoughts wandered to Gabe, and he tripped, just missing a sharp rock. Daniel knew from researching this prison that if he allowed the guards to get him beyond the first check-point, they'd be good as dead—the walking dead. Daniel played out what he had to do to save them. He counted the seconds while the base of the piped dome in front of him opened up. A doorway leading into a dark abyss teased him. The first guard went through, and he peeked behind him in time to catch Faulk's jaw drop. Michael's steely expression clashed with his.

Daniel ran through his memory, calculating what he was up against. Different levels for a diverse type of prisoners. Daniel figured it was mostly underground, but now he knew parts of the structure were above ground. Sewer systems ran throughout the place. But to get to Gabe in medical, they'd have to get that information from a guard.

Daniel was pushed forward and entered into what he'd imagine the pit of hell would smell like. Rotten flesh, spoiled food and fire. The elevator walls were uneven and appeared to be made out of carved rock. Thin illuminated blue lines trimmed the ceiling and gave the place a bluish tint. The guards snorted at them and pushed them against the back wall. Daniel eyed the others, hoping they'd get his signal to watch him. Michael responded with a subtle nod and Faulk's eyebrow went up. Jade smirked and studied the guard in front of her.

After several minutes, the elevator stopped. Daniel eyed the lit up symbols on the wall and realized the language was Jergin, from the planet where the Warden was from. Most of the guards were from the slave region of that planet, so Daniel assumed that when the Warden created this penal colony, it was easier for him to bring his own species with him.

Daniel watched the motion of the guard's finger and the risen alien symbols on the wall. He noted that there were two lower levels that the elevator could take them. The mines where they made the prisoners work couldn't be accessed from this location. His finger slid in the hidden slit in his pants along the seam at his hip. The guard in front of him turned around. Sweat beaded on Daniel's forehead. He stilled and controlled his breathing—a lesson his father had taught him long ago. After sizing him up a moment, the guard turned back around. Daniel resumed sliding the metal string from the slit within the seam in the back of his pants. With his arms behind him, he looped each end of it around the forefinger of both hands. He was ready.

"Out!" the guard in front of Daniel called, not sparing Daniel a glimpse.

With lightning speed, Daniel looped the wired weapon around the guard's neck, then tugged it tightly, sawing it back and forth through the thick skin of the guard's neck.

Michael's arm snaked around the other guard and gutted the thick beast, then whipped around and stabbed the other in the neck before the guard could push the alert button on the elevator.

Jade stabbed a guard in the back of the neck and Faulk finished him off by jabbing the clubbed weapon into the guard's open mouth.

Nickel weaved in and out of the foray grabbing weapons before he warned, "More are coming!"

Michael ripped the backpack off Daniel. "This is mine, and so is he!" He snatched Faulk by the hair, pointed his knife under Faulk's neck, and dragged a struggling Faulk down the rock covered hall towards the guards.

Daniel lunged for them.

Nickel screamed, "No, you won't make it!"

More guards were closing in. Daniel skidded to a stop as Michael and Faulk slipped out of view

"Get back in the elevator!" Daniel ran into the elevator.

Nickel handed him a metal tubed device. "We have to cut through the bottom!"

"Right! Jade, close that door." Daniel pressed the button and activated the cutting device Nickel gave him.

"No…no…no!" Jade pounded the buttons on the wall. "Nothings working!"

Daniel's jaw clenched. He was almost finished cutting a circle big enough for them to fit through. "Help her, Nickel! Remember what Dad taught us."

Nickel worked his fingers with ease across the flat lit up panel.

Jade's stilled and stepped back. "I'll kill some of them." Smoothly, she slid darts off her belt. "Poisonous and quiet." She flung several darts toward the group of guards that was closing in. Their thick skin bubbled. The pupils of their eyes turned deep purple, then released gushing white blood that covered their faces.

Within seconds, the doors closed. "I did it!" Nickel jumped up and down.

"Good kid, just in time." Daniel stood and stomped on the metal circle he'd created in the floor. "Jump down. Nickel first, then you, Jade."

Nickel rushed over and jumped on the hanging cable. Jade followed. Daniel aimed the cylindrical tool onto the door and melted the center together to close the hole just as the banging started.

A grin slipped to his lips, as he smoothly jumped to follow Jade.

23

Daniel was pissed. There was no doubt in his mind now that Michael had come with them for the sole purpose of retrieving the treasure. His fingers tightened on the thick cable as he shimmied downward into the section of the jail he knew held the low level prisoners—the slaves. The upper level held the most dangerous beings in the universe, and there was no way Daniel wanted to even risk going where they were. That area would be heavily guarded.

"There," Daniel pointed to one of the small alcoves in the wall, "rest there."

Nickel swayed the cable over and hopped into the alcove with grace that belied his small size. Jade followed. Daniel held on tightly to the cable and waited for them to make room for him. "Don't move." He jumped into the middle.

Daniel made himself comfortable between them. "I gotta call Franz." He fiddled with the communicator lodged in his ear. His eyes shuttered closed as he quickly prayed that the communications barrier would lift enough for Franz to pick up his signal. A static-filled transmission came in.

"Daniel? Where the hell is Gabe?" Franz's deep static laced voice yelled.

"I don't know—I need to find him, soon. And Michael, he's gone rogue."

"What the hell? What do you mean?" Franz demanded.

"He went for the Warden's treasure. I know it. I have to stop him or we all will be dead. He even kidnapped Faulk!" Daniel gritted out.

"Why would he want to take Faulk anywhere with him? I'm sorry, man, but your cousin is worthless as a Zukar. I'm working on disabling the security beacon," Franz growled. "They didn't make it easy. So lay low, stay off the main floors."

"Got it. Can you send me coordinates to where the Zukar records state the treasure is held?" Daniel knew Franz would have to break into the main computer the Zukar used to plan their jobs, but if anyone could do it – Franz could.

"You're shittin' me, right?" Franz sounded ticked.

"No, it's where Michael's heading." He had to find out where it was located from someone. Someone who's got an agenda that might not include the rest of us surviving. Daniel should have known Michael was up to something. Since they'd been on the ship together, Michael had hidden himself away, studying maps, the planet Uukin, and anything he could find on the Warden. When Daniel asked him why he was doing Franz's job, Michael had ignored his question and went to his room.

"Fine, I'll follow Michael's footsteps on this, but I'd guess the treasure would be in the Warden's quarters, it's one of the most heavily guarded parts of the jail." Franz's voice faded out and the communication went dead.

Jade tapped Daniel's shoulder. "You really think Michael's that crazy? Why would he want to do that alone? What would he want with the warden's treasure anyway?"

"Once a thief always a thief, I guess." Daniel ground his teeth. "But what I still don't get is why he even bothered to take Faulk. He hates my cousin."

Nickel released a sigh. "He took him because Faulk stole some gold egg or something from him. I don't know what it does, but Faulk told him you had it. Michael didn't believe him."

"Wait. Faulk stole something from Michael, then blamed it on me? Why?"

Nickel shrugged. "I don't know, I think to prove to Michael that he fit in with us. But they had a fight just before we got off the ship and I don't think Faulk even remembered he had it."

"Yeah, but then Michael 'saved' ya'll and I bet he wanted the thing back." Daniel cursed and leaned forward on his knees.

"He didn't save us. I begged him to. He just wanted what Faulk took from him." Nickel got a blank look in his eyes. "I didn't think he hated us so much till now." His voice had grown quiet.

Jade rubbed Nickel's back. "Michael doesn't hate you or anyone. He's just the quiet type. He was harsh with me when I was little. Zero patience is his problem."

Nickel frowned. "Is something wrong with you? You talk funny."

Daniel elbowed him. "She got poisoned and her memory is vague. Jade doesn't remember me."

Nickel smiled up at Jade. "What about me? You always sing to me when no one's around."

Jade laughed. "No, I don't now, but I want to. I always wanted a baby brother to boss around."

"You used to tell me that all the time, so maybe you do – like a reflex or something." Nickel winked at her. "A little?"

She shook her head. "Sorry, not a bit. But I'm remembering more and more every second so the more we are together, the sooner I'll recall the songs I sang to you in secret."

The communication device in his ear beeped making Daniel's hand jerk. "Franz? What you got?"

"A jacked up map, but it'll help a little. And more bad-ass news." Franz didn't sound happy.

"Nothing I can't handle, I need to get to Gabe. Did you get a signal on him?" Daniel frowned.

"The only way you'll be able to find him is to deactivate the security system located in the Warden's lair. Yeah…and I said lair. From what the Zukar has recorded, that bastard is sick, and keeps the security system locked in his personal quarters. He's hiding something."

"How is killing the system going to help me get Gabe?"

"It will weaken the security shields around the lower part of the jail. He's probably in processing. Apparently, they tag incoming slaves, and he fits in the slave category because he was captured and he's under the age of twenty-one. They have level five criminals there next to the mines where the slaves work, but you don't want to mess with those screwed-up creatures. They are real criminals who are a danger to anyone. Whatever you do—DO NOT RELEASE them! You do, we are all screwed. Those things are world destroyers, loyal to no one."

"Send me what you've got." Daniel clenched his jaw. "I'll get to Michael and Faulk then save Gabe's ass."

"You better. 'Sides, you know you always liked a challenge. Just like your dad." Franz faded out.

Yeah, just like his father. Daniel wanted to make his father proud, but his heart throbbed knowing he'd failed time and time again. Still, if he could save Faulk, punch some sense into Michael, and grab Gabe, he would succeed. At least he would—this one time.

24

Michael pushed Faulk forward with his gun. The stone formed door that led to the sewage and waste areas beneath ground was slightly ajar. Taking a cursory search around the waste closet, he swallowed a gulp of foul air. "Hurry up and open it before I throw you to the guards."

Faulk fumbled with the latch that closed the wood hatch on the floor. "What is in here? Do you even know? We should've stayed with the others." He shivered, apparently disgusted.

"Shut up! I'm sick of your bullshit. If we get killed, you and your stupid cousin will be the reason." Michael nudged the butt of his gun against Faulk's temple. "Hurry, they're near."

The rumbling of multiple feet scurried on the outside of the closet. Michael was able to sneak them into one of the locked waste closets with the Zukar code key the Sira Zukar gave him as part of the deal made to get the Warden's treasure and kill Daniel.

"There, it's opened. Now what?" Faulk frowned at him with hunched shoulders.

Even though Faulk tried to appear nonchalant, Michael noticed Faulk's nose crinkled at the foul odor.

Michael smiled, couldn't help it really, the more time he spent with Faulk, the more he realized he hated the guy. Hated him and his cousin Daniel for bringing their family's screwed-up litany of problems onto him. Michael wished his father, Bry, had never even met Daniel's father, Rayne.

Faulk's eyes grew wide. "You don't expect me to get in there, do you?"

Michael lifted his foot and kicked Faulk on the side of his face. "Yep."

Faulk fell backwards into the murky waters.

Michael tucked his gun back on his belt then slid down into the hole while pulling the lid over with his other hand. Taking a deep breath, and holding it, Michael jumped down the twelve feet. The putrid smell forced the yell in his throat stuck behind closed lips. Humid air seemed to press his skin and Faulk pinch his nose closed just before hitting the thick moving waters.

Faulk was coughing and wiping gritty brown water off his face. "What is this stuff?"

"Shit and other waste." Michael walked past Faulk and sloshed through the two feet of thick, dirty water. The place seemed to go on forever. Low and high ceilings with no patterns, but sitting at least six or more feet above the moving liquid. He glanced over his shoulder at the daft prisoner and snorted.

"You're kidding, right? Why the hell would you want to go this way when it was safer to stay with the others?" Faulk spun around at the sound of more rushing water, then turned to jog up to Michael.

Michael shook his head and pivoted around, walking faster. "No, I'm not. We aren't going with Daniel. He didn't have what I wanted.

But I'm sure you do. Since you don't want to give it to me, I'm taking you with me."

"Why is it so important to you?" Faulk caught up to him. He shivered.

"It's my business, but it'll unlock the Warden's treasure for me. And if I don't return with it, none of us will live." Michael's shoulders straightened. He studied Faulk who was crinkling his nose against the smell while eyeing sticky goo that seemed to glow on their clothes in the dark tunnel of rushing dense substance.

"I don't understand why you didn't just tell everyone that's what you wanted to do. Daniel would've listened." Faulk walked easily alongside Michael, now seemingly accustomed to the foul smell.

"Because Daniel had fed my brothers a pound of bull about changing our lives from being Zukar. I couldn't risk it. Him—us— good guys?" Michael shook his head and laughed, "Yeah right, all I ever wanted was this life. I'd been raised to be a thief, even made it to the first tier of up-and-coming assassins for special jobs, and your cousin messed that up for me – for all of us."

"So you were faking it on the ship? You acted like you wanted this. We all did." Faulk slicked back a long piece of his straight black hair off his face.

"I never said I wanted that. I just agreed to come here." Michael stopped and placed his hands on his hips. "You ready to spill where you hid my gold egg? If you do, I'll let you go now."

Faulk frowned at him. "Go where? I'm safer with you than doing this myself. Besides, I don't have it." He shrugged.

Michael sized him up. "You do. Stop lying. You've lied to everyone since the day you set foot on Merwin, and you're lying now."

Faulk scratched his head. "I'm not telling you where it is until we meet up with Daniel. You agreed to get me to him safely, but you reneged on that. Knowledge about the egg is the only insurance that keeps me alive."

Michael smirked. "You think I'd kill you after I get what I want?"

Faulk gave him a wry smile. "I have a strong feeling you will. You did say you were a thief and a murderer, and isn't killing and lying what thieves do best?"

"Humph, I'll take you with me, but before I let you out of this sewer, I'll take what's mine, even if I have to cut you open to do it." Michael turned away from him, disgusted. He'd have to let Faulk live a little longer, even if he did get that key from him—he wanted Daniel, needed a person's death, their blood, to unlock the Warden's treasure. He'd been told by the Sira Zukar to make sure Daniel would be the sacrifice.

25

Daniel held Jade's hand and nodded at Nickel. "When we go below there, it's going to be a fight, but we have to run into the room down on the lower level. Life or death. You with me?"

Jade nudged him with her elbow. "Is that the only way? I don't want to lose Nickel."

Again. Daniel tried to suppress the accusation that sprang to mind at Jade's concern. He didn't want to bring that up to her. Part of him wished she'd never remember the way he treated her earlier. But he had to trust her now. Had to. "I'll go first, fight a path for us through the guards since Franz hopefully disabled their coms unit that would alert the other guards to our breach."

"I hope it worked," Nickel uttered while biting his nails.

"Lucky for u, the Warden's a conceited bastard who's never been challenged before. Also, he's paranoid and never lets anyone deliver supplies here that he can't make himself. So in some ways, Uukin is limited in security compared to other places the Zukar have broken into. But the fact that this place is deadly, and the Warden can unleash the Level 5's out into the universe means no one has felt the need to breach this planet. Not only that, very few people know of the Warden's treasure." Daniel squeezed Jade's hand.

Jade frowned. "Then why does the Zukar know of it?"

"Good question, considering they are supposedly against the King of Merwin sending their young members here as slaves when their parents die." Daniel's tightened his jaw. The more he thought about it, the more the Sira Zukar having intimate knowledge of the Warden and Uukin irritated him. It was starting to feel like the Sira Zukar and the Warden had an agreement of sorts. If the children of rich Zukars were removed, the Sira Zukar and his officials could claim the parent's treasure troves and steal the riches from their own members who'd served them for years.

"Daniel, what's wrong? You look angry." Jade slid her hand from his. "And you're squeezing my hand."

"Sorry. I was thinking." Daniel flicked on his com device and prayed Franz answered.

Franz's deep voice skipped through the fuzzy transmission. "Speak."

"Why would Michael want the Warden's treasure? Do you remember anything from when the Sira Zukar captured and tortured you?" Daniel's fist opened and closed, and his blood drummed through him with his anger at the Sira Zukar's possible deceit.

"I got my ass kicked, got stabbed…oh, and whipped. Did I mention my nails being pulled off?" Franz screamed. "Need I say more?"

"Yeah, like how did you get away? Did you and Michael make a deal with the Sira Zukar?" Daniel released a growl deep in his throat. "Did Michael?"

Franz hesitated. "I don't know. Maybe. But I was knocked out before they started in on Michael's torture. The next thing I remember was being woken up on your ship in the healing machine and told by you that we had to get off of Merwin or we'd die."

Daniel closed his eyes and used his finger and thumb to rub his eyelids. "Damn. Michael wasn't in the shape you were in. He had some bruises, a broken rib or two, and some contusions but that's it."

Franz's connection was lost.

Daniel groaned. It was highly likely that the Sira Zukar made a deal with Michael to save Franz's life. And Daniel would bet his mother's necklace on the fact that the deal would include that he and Nickel never made it back to Merwin alive. Rayne's treasure trove was one of the most coveted ones on the entire planet – besides Bry's, Gabe's father. Daniel had to get to Michael before he did something stupid.

"What is it?" Jade asked quietly. She gently laid a hand on Daniel's shoulder.

"Nothing, just the reason Michael's acting so irrational." He shrugged. "Let's go save his stupid ass." Daniel jumped and grabbed hold of the cable. Looking up, Daniel instructed, "Put Nickel in the middle."

Jade nodded at him. "You want me to cover the rear?" She smiled.

"You okay with that?" He shimmied down a bit to make room for Nickel. His muscles twitched in his neck and back, but he was used to the bite of pain. It came with the job. Besides, he'd been trained to tolerate intense pain when necessary.

"Perfectly." She winked at him. "Let's go save my brother from himself." With ease, she followed Nickel down.

Daniel balanced on the towline and looped the excess around his foot as he steadied himself. He held tightly to the cable with one hand while the other dug a small, flat, clear device from his belt. His eyebrows creased as he secured it to the elevator door. Franz had given him a visual map of this section but there were details missing. He'd figure his way out – had too, since failure wasn't an option. Daniel tapped the clear disc and a mirror image of the hall in front of him illuminated on the elevator door as if a movie was playing on a screen. Guards shuffled down the hall, which appeared to have three doors— two on one side and one at the end.

"Damn!" Daniel's finger pointed at the door at the end of the hall.

"What?" Nickel gulped.

"Franz didn't tell me about the other two doors, and the one at the end of the hall we have to get to is locked."

"And that means?" Jade asked.

"It means we have to fight to get to it. Even though Franz was able to interrupt the security beacons, they can turn on any moment. We'll be in deep crap if they do." Daniel yanked off the device and the picture instantly disappeared. He stuffed it in his belt and extracted a small curved metal tool that he slid on his bent forefinger like a ring with a tiny crowbar on the end.

"I've got some darts that spit smoke if that'll help," Jade whispered. She ran her hand over the belt that wrapped around her shoulder and connected at her waist.

"It will. And Nickel, you're gonna need this." Daniel pulled out Nickel's slingshot and gave it to him.

"Yeah!" Nickel flicked it in his wrist.

"Nickel, whatever happens, stay right behind me. Get your weapons ready." Daniel used the tool on his finger to pry the door open and hoped the hall was still clear. The doors swung open before he could brace it, just as a guard stepped out into the opening. Daniel bit back a curse. He charged the guard, his feet slipping slightly on the smooth floor. Sliding his finger across the trigger, Daniel grinned and released a shot.

Its mouth opened to roar. Daniel's laser burned the back of its mouth before it could release any sound. It dropped to its knees. But another guard barreled through the opened door. Daniel grunted, and bent his forefinger in challenge, ready for a second attack.

"Ya!" Jade rained multiple darts in every eye on the guard's angry face.

It gurgled, and its thick fingers grasped its neck. Smoke simmered from its open mouth. *Pop!* A flash of fire licked through its teeth and each dart expelled a thick spray of smoke into the hall. Its head blew up with a wet quiet splat. Daniel ducked and slid through the gooey flesh racing to the door.

"C'mon!" His eyes watered from the smoke filling the hall. He slipped a tiny tube from his belt and pressed it against the thick knob of the door. The lock picker slid a small piece of metal into the cylinder-shaped keyhole. Daniel was sweating, hoping that more guards weren't alerted.

Nickel smacked at his back, coughing. "What'd she put in that?"

"A bit of explosives, herbs for added smoke effect, and poison. The best quiet bomb you can create." Jade tapped his arm. "I closed the door they came out of."

"Good thinking…this will only be one more min—" The lock clicked, and Daniel grinned. "We're in."

26

Faulk swallowed down a gag. His eyes never left Michael's back as they trudged through the murky water filled with glowing waste. He didn't have any doubt about it – Michael hated him, and would probably kill him soon if he didn't think of something to put off the inevitable further. The only thing Faulk knew was keeping him alive was the flat, blood-colored ruby he'd tucked in the hidden slit of his pants.

"Hurry up, if you want to stay alive. They have creatures in here that eat the waste. And you – are definitely a piece of waste," Michael chuckled.

Faulk shivered. "Will this take us to where Daniel is?" He knew asking Michael questions would anger him even more, but he hoped it would cause Michael to slip up. To tell him any clue to where they were going and what Michael was really planning for them. "How do you know Daniel and the others even made it?"

"You talk too much." Michael stopped, ran a hand through his thick curly hair. "I need to meet your cousin, but I've also got to get somewhere." He started walking again.

"But do you think he'll be alright? I thought the Zukar way was to stay in pairs." Faulk eyed Michael as he tracked faster through the waist-deep liquid. "You can't think Jade would be able to help him?"

"No, but Daniel's good. He'll make it." Michael turned around, his angry expression open and heated as he sized up Faulk with his eyes. "He always was the *good* guy. Just like his father. Funny thing was, his father made a mistake that caused my dad to pay for it. And history just seems to keep repeating itself. My family is, once again, paying the damn price for Daniel's screw-ups." He pushed Faulk's chest. "But if you give me what I've been asking for, I'll consider the debt – paid."

Faulk shrugged and tried to stay calm. "How can what I took on the ship help you?"

Michael lifted an eyebrow. "Don't play me like a fool." He leaned in closer, "You try to act like the joker, the funny man, but I know your game. I know you tried to sabotage what Daniel and my family does for a living, but you don't get us or what we stand for – and never will."

"I get you, and Daniel. But as I see it, being with the Zukar hasn't worked out too good for any of you. The minute you can't be *used* by them, they what…" Faulk smirked. "Oh yeah, sell you out to the King of Merwin who wants to ship you all to this planet to become slaves to the Warden of Uukin. To mine what? Oh yeah," he snapped his fingers, "some substance that comes from an unknown source. I'm sure it supplies a powerful energy base to distant warring planets. Those that are slowly making their way to Earth to destroy all the inhabitants there – your heritage – human people will die. All because, this prick of a Warden has been allowed to deal death only because he happens to imprison Level 5 world eaters in his prison."

Michael jerked his chin up. "So you been studying? Well, that's all you're good at."

"No, I'm good at caring about my actions. Like seeing that you getting what you want from me can cause your family death. Seems like that isn't Daniel's fault, it's yours."

Michael's expression turned furious. "You are lucky I can't kill you until I get what I want. You're useless."

Faulk gulped, and straightened his shoulders. "Apparently not, since I got something you need. And obviously, real bad." He inhaled. "Now, if you want it from me – there's something you have to agree to."

Michael smirked. "You getting some cojones now, growing some courage to come up against me?" He hit his chest.

"It was always there, you were just too much of a dumbass to see it." Faulk grinned, forcing back the pain in his leg, chest and face from the beatings Michael gave him.

Michael grabbed Faulk by the shirt and lifted him up on his toes. "Don't push me."

"I'm not trying to, but if you want me to hand over to you the only thing that's keeping me alive, then we've got to get to Daniel." Faulk forced himself not to blink or give away his deception. "Trust me, he has what you want, and if we do this together, we'll all get out of here safe. And you have my permission to kick my ass after we get the treasure. But saving Gabe and Jade has to be our top priority. If Gabe gets sent to the slave mines, he's good as dead."

Michael shook his head. "He'll live. They'll want him to work. But when I get my property from you, it will set everyone free."

Faulk didn't hold back the look of horror he knew spilled on his face. "That'll mean that the Level 5s will be free. They'll destroy this planet and any other planet close enough for them to escape to."

Michael released Faulk and shrugged. "Not my problem. Zukar don't save people, we take what we want and get the hell out." He started to turn around.

Faulk grabbed his shirt. "You can't do that! I won't let you — Daniel won't let you."

Michael slapped Faulk's hand away. "Then use that treasure your uncle stole from the Zukar, the pakeet, to replenish this world and contain the Level 5's. That's not my problem."

"It is, because the closest planet to Uukin is Merwin, the planet your parents are residing on as we speak." Faulk's eyebrow went up.

Michael sighed. "Maybe, but if I know your cousin, he'll figure out where I'm heading, and trust me, he'll be there." He pivoted around. "You just better hope I have the patience to make sure you're there too."

Faulk released the breath he'd been holding. Lifting his foot to follow, he relaxed a little. He'd stood up to Michael all on a bluff. His finger absently rubbed the seam on his pants that hid what Michael wanted. Thank God, he bought the lie. Bluffing was never something he'd thought he was good at. Aw hell, he bluffed all the time, but to be able to make Michael believe it…now that was skill. He grinned. Another hour, he'd stayed alive for another hour.

Something slithered against his leg. Faulk gulped. Maybe, he better not count the entire hour.

27

No fear. Just do. Daniel's father's words drummed in his head. Times like this, he missed him, and regretted at one time, he'd thought he hated Rayne. Daniel opened the door and adrenaline, like a welcome drug, filled his veins. Swallowing, he held up a hand. He didn't know how Jade or Nickel would handle what he saw in the room. The floor wasn't like any he'd ever seen. Two-inch spikes protruded from every square foot. It was littered with body parts and strewn with clothes. The pace of his heart went up a notch. On the ceiling were rounded metal bars wide enough for them to hold onto.

A discarded flat square metal panel leaned against the door. And the smell; he never thought this hell could smell worse than it had so far, but he was wrong.

"What is it?" Jade whispered.

"Nothing. You and Nickel have to go first. You, then him." Daniel anxiously used his finger to play with a metal button on his belt. A roped wire extended out and latched onto the first metal bar. "I hope this holds," he muttered.

The drumming of blood in his ears and the raised hairs on his neck were for Nickel. His father had trained Nickel too, but not even Daniel had been placed in this type of challenge before he'd turned twelve. Daniel waved away some of the faltering smoke and realized that they didn't have much time.

Jade grabbed the roped wire and held tight as she leaned forward. "It's okay." Her gaze collided with Daniel's. "You have me?"

"Yeah, just speed up. I don't know how much time we have." Dribbles of sweat beaded his forehead. He waited until Jade grabbed the first bar on the ceiling and patted Nickel on his back. "You think you can make it?"

Nickel's grin burst wide, reminding Daniel of the smile his mother gave him when she was alive. "Piece of cake!" He shimmied up the intertwined wires with ease and slid behind Jade, who'd moved about four bars ahead.

Daniel pushed the switch on his belt and the hook released. While the rope collapsed into his belt he leaned over and grabbed the flat metal panel he'd spied earlier. He tossed it below the first bar. Cracking his neck to the side, Daniel measured the distance with his eyes and jumped onto the metal piece with light feet. He balanced for a moment, released a breath, then pressed the button on his belt and waited for the hook on his rope to catch onto the bar.

Jade hesitated and looked back at him. "You..."

Daniel shook his head. "Keep going, I'll catch up." The hook caught and with a heave, he climbed up the thick wire and grasped the bar. Holding the bar with one hand, he balanced his weight and pushed the button on his belt to release the rope. Like climbing monkey bars when he was a kid, he swung himself with precision and speed from bar to bar behind Jade.

Click. Click. Click. The door from which they'd come locked closed.

"Damn. It's a timer," Daniel muttered, and a slow hissing sound seeped from the floor of the room followed by a gas. "Hold your breath."

"What is it?" Jade stopped with both hands squeezing the bar.

"Don't stop! Hold your breath till you get to the door," Daniel ground out trying not to inhale the sickly sweet scent that filled the room. Holding his breath, he doubled his time and came up behind Nickel. One more jump and he held onto the side of the bar with his chest to Nickel's back. "Be still," he whispered, releasing some precious air as his muscles relaxed in release when the toxic gas, expelling from the cracks, stopped.

Click. Click. The mutilated pieces of flesh on the floor dissolved. Then the floor shifted and the liquid waste slid into slits around the spiked edges.

Daniel took a tentative sniff. It seemed free of the sickly sweet smell. He swallowed. "Jade, I'm going around you in case one of those bastards is waiting on the other side of the door."

"What are we going to do when we get out?" She steadied herself.

Daniel grasped just above her hands and balanced himself against her. "Hold still, you're worst than Nickel," he chuckled.

"Humph, I don't think so. I'm a girl, 'kay, and having you this close seems kinda weird."

Daniel smiled when subconsciously, Jade leaned back into him, so he landed a soft kiss on the base of her neck. Jade gave him a shaky smile. "Sorry about that." Daniel balanced on one hand then reached around her to hop to the next bar. "I couldn't help myself."

Tink. Tink. Tink.

"Aww freak, what now?" Nickel whined.

Daniel steadied himself and counted the remaining bars. The bar he held tingled under his fingers just before it shocked him. "Hold on!"

"Oww!" Jade shrieked, before one of her hands released the bar. "Electric shocks."

"Damn." Daniel held tight as another shock came. His eyes fell to Nickel.

"Don't worry about me, Dad taught me to fight pain." Nickel frowned and released a gasp when another shock hit, a lone tear slid down his cheek.

"Move faster. Jade focus your mind on getting out. Push the pain back. Don't think about it." Another shock hit his hand, stronger than the one before and his fingers trembled for a moment.

He kept moving. "C'mon keep up. We can do this." Daniel hoped using his voice would help them. He hated risking being heard, but he wanted them to live. The flat metal platform in front of the door beckoned him like a mirage. His heart beat faster, adrenaline kicked up so high he didn't flinch when another electric shock hit. He shook it off. Expelling a breath, he couldn't help the smirk that blossomed on his lips. Daniel leaped with ease and landed on the platform in front of the door.

"Al…most." Nickel jumped and landed with a slide in front of Daniel. "Here." He laughed. "Easy."

Jade swung forward and leaped.

Daniel opened his arms and caught her. Pulling her close to him in a hug he landed a kiss before she could fight him. "Safe."

She leaned back. "Not from you. Stop stealing kisses." Jade punched him in the arm.

"I can't help it. I'm just glad to be alive. Glad we all are." Daniel sighed. "Now, to challenge that." He turned towards the door and shrugged. "Get your weapons ready. Your brother tipped me off on a way out of this next hallway alive. I'll fight off any guards but you run like hell to the end of the hall, then climb up into the venting system. Don't let them see you do it."

Nickel frowned. "What about you?"

Daniel ruffled Nickel's hair. "I'll be there. Don't wait for me. Get in and keep going till I catch up."

Jade's expression was skeptical. "What if you don't?"

He grinned at her. "I always do."

28

Michael didn't bother to check on Faulk. Why should he? He didn't care if the screw-up lived or died. He just wanted this crap over. He wanted his life back before Daniel came and ripped it up. Now his home and his family were at risk thanks to Daniel's carelessness, the selfish son-of-a bastard. All Daniel cared about was what he wanted, honoring his dead, dumbass father.

"Did you hear me?" Faulk's insistent whine came from behind.

"What now?" Michael exhaled.

"Your father and my uncle Rayne were best friends, right? Since when?"

Michael would've kept silent, except if he was honest with himself, he wanted someone to talk to. Even if that someone was Daniel's cocky cousin. "Yeah, and?"

"Doesn't that mean they wanted the same thing from both of you?"

Michael stopped, pivoted around and frowned with his hands on his hip. "No."

Faulk slowly nodded his head up and down. "Yes." He took a tentative step closer. "Just...I."

"Hell—no!" Michael's muscles tensed and he saw red with anger. Yes, anger that simmered deep within him. It kept him on his game, helped him survive and become the Zukar he'd been trained to be.

"Yes."

Michael stepped forward and grabbed the front of Faulk's shirt. "No."

"Just hear me out, okay?" A hesitant smile bloomed on Faulk's face. He struggled a bit, moving his shoulders from side to side.

Releasing Faulk with a push, Michael growled. "Speak. Fool." He couldn't believe he was giving the idiot a chance, but what else did he have to do? Until he got the gold egg the dumbass stole from him, he had to put up with him.

"Look." Faulk gulped. "Your father talked to Daniel for a while before we left. He made it clear that he and Rayne wanted the same things."

"Bullshit." Michael turned away.

"Seriously, I'm not lying to you. Rayne gave his life trying to get Daniel and Nickel to turn away from the Zukar. They didn't want to do the crimes anymore."

Michael stopped. "Nothing new with that sorry-assed excuse for bailing out on the Zukar."

"Bailing out? You can't be that stupid."

Michael jerked around, making the thick, sludgy water splash. "You calling me stupid? You are the dumb one here. Remember, your life is the one I've got in the palm of my hands."

"True, you can kill me, leave me, slice me into pieces and serve me up to the fish here – but you need me. So give me a chance to explain." Faulk's jaw set and he blinked several times as though he was trying to gain some courage. "I know you won't kill me. You might have had to do that when you were training as a Zukar, but I don't think you'd do it just for fun."

Michael ignored the slight dip in the guard he'd put up from years of training. "My father wanted this for me. He was the first to train me and my brothers. Hell, he's the one who told Rayne to escape with Haden to Merwin in the first place and started their lives as renowned thieves. If my father hadn't met Haden when your uncle Rayne was accused of robbing that store on Earth, then they both would've been in some Earth jail."

"No. Haden was the reason they were stealing anyway. Did your father ever tell you the entire story?" Faulk started to relax and crossed his arms.

"None of it, but I figured it out." Michael eyed Faulk, hating to admit he'd wanted to know what happened. He'd even asked his father. But his father only told him it was a story he wanted to forget.

"My father and Daniel explained what happened. Haden had come to Earth on some type of job or training for the Zukar. One of the things he had to do was recruit new members. Their numbers were low. Haden and my uncle Rayne met up at some club or hangout on Earth and Haden asked my uncle for a ride. They picked up your father and while on the way home, Haden asked them to stop. While they waited outside, Haden robbed the store, killed two guys and jumped into the car with my uncle."

"Go on." Michael's heart thumped in his chest. He'd heard parts of the story, but things never really added up 'til now. Maybe Faulk was telling the truth, but maybe not.

"My uncle had called my father. My dad tried to convince Rayne to stay on Earth, to tell what Haden had done. But your father explained about the murder and that Haden had friends, dangerous friends."

"What has that got to do with the fact that now we are fugitives from the Zukar?" Michael knew there were other Zukar with Haden when he went to Earth, that part of the story wasn't new. But the revelation that Haden orchestrated everything made Michael sick to his stomach. He wouldn't put it past his father's old friend, especially after what he'd endured during his torture and agreement to kill Daniel, but it was hard to swallow.

"Everything." Faulk's shoulders sagged. Frustrated, he swiped a hand through is spiked black hair.

Michael snorted. "You're uncle is the cause of that. Even if he was murdered. Rayne stole a treasure that he was sent to give to the Sira Zukar. But he never turned it in. All of the Zukar were on high alert because your uncle tried to say the treasure was lost. Strange how it ended up inside you and Daniel."

"It didn't happen like that. Rayne had to protect the pakeet. This treasure isn't controllable. It was eating your world, Merwin, up from the inside out. Anyone that touched it, without knowing or understanding its power, would poison its purpose."

Michael lifted an eyebrow. "And Rayne didn't know that? You can't tell me that your uncle didn't plan to use it against the Zukar. To give it to his son."

"He didn't!" Faulk balled his fist. "He hid it to save your world – and *your* father helped him."

"You lie," Michael's voice was low and deadly.

"No, I'm not lying. That's why he sent you with Daniel and us. It was the only way to protect you. He told Daniel while I was standing next to him that he and Rayne knew the risk for withholding that treasure. But you have to understand, they became and stayed Zukar because they didn't have a choice – at least they didn't think they did until my uncle found the pakeet, and realized that he could change his life."

Michael waved an angry hand. "Pah! Where did that get your uncle? Dead, murdered in cold blood in his own home. And where did that get my father? Nowhere. We are on the run and my parents are…" He let out a fierce growl. "Just shut up. I'm done talking." He turned and stormed off. Water splashed behind him and he could hear Faulk's heavy breathing and spraying of water as he tried to keep up.

"You can fix this. We can fix it. Just catch up with Daniel and we can save Gabe then leave." Faulk yanked on Michael's vest.

Michael jerked away. "I came here for something, and I'm not leaving without it." He turned cold eyes down on Faulk, hate, anger and helplessness tickled his chest. "There's no choice for us now. Rayne started this – I'll finish it and save my family."

Faulk's eyes widened, his hand trembled, and he let go of Michael's shirt.

At that moment, Michael released it, the anger, the hate, the jealousy that he'd felt for Daniel. It oozed from his skin and from his eyes that nailed Faulk. "You touch me again. I'll kill you."

29

Gun drawn, Daniel charged into the hall, shooting one of the guards on sight. Nickel sprinted past him and raised his slingshot to knock an eye out of another. Daniel slid to his feet, tripped Nickel's victim, and stomped onto its neck.

"Hurry!" Daniel slammed his back against an opening door. The guard he'd felled earlier started to rise. Daniel delivered several shots to its head as Jade lifted Nickel to the vent.

Thump. Thump. Daniel slid a few inches as another guard shoved on the door. He searched around for something to barricade it closed and smiled at the unconscious guards around him. He risked bending to pull the one at his feet closer to the door. Then he spun around, fired several rounds at the door's lock and wedged the body in place.

"I'm coming! Jade, blow something up!" Daniel raced to the vent, Jade bent over with Nickel to help him up.

She twisted away and tossed a dart down when the door opened. In a flash and with a pop, smoke filled the corridor, just as Daniel slid the vent closed.

"Go! Go! Go!" Daniel pushed Nickel and Jade forward.

"Daniel, the guards—are they going to call others?" Jade asked as she slowed down.

"Let's rest a minute." Daniel stopped and leaned against the rounded wall of the vent. Thankful for the darkness around them he gazed down. He tapped on the communicator on his hip and glanced at the cryptic message from Franz.

Jade leaned over his shoulder. "What's he say?"

Daniel turned his head slightly and gave her a quick kiss.

"Yuck! Get a room," Nickel snickered.

Daniel chuckled at Jade's shocked expression. "He said there's not much further to go. He's suppressing their alarm signals, but it's getting hard for him to do it for long."

"Really? Then how much further?" Jade said, instinctively moving closer to Daniel's steady warmth.

"A ways yet, and if we stay up here till we get above the Warden's quarters, we should be relatively fine…" Daniel swallowed, looking ahead at some of the lit spots in the vent where there was no covering, where they could be exposed.

"But Faulk and Michael—which way did they go?" Nickel asked while rubbing a jagged rock on his pants leg and fitting it inside his slingshot.

"Only one other option, and that's not a safe path, but knowing Michael, he'd take it just to piss Faulk off." Daniel snorted and laid an arm around Jade who didn't flinch this time.

"You really think Michael would try to steal this treasure from the Warden alone?" Jade relaxed a bit in his arms.

"Yeah, I think he made a deal with our crooked Sira Zukar. And it makes me wonder why we haven't heard from your parents since we escaped Merwin."

"We escaped?" She sat up. "Why?"

"Because my father stole a coveted treasure that no other thief in the universe had been able to get to. He also earned it from the hands of the alien race that created the device to destroy weak worlds and to replenish and build new worlds."

Nickel laid on Jade's other side and bent his legs. "But my dad hid the pakeet, and meant for only me and Daniel to protect it – from everyone."

Daniel moved a wayward curl off Jade's face. "Then when he got murdered, we – you and us with Faulk, retrieved the treasure, only thinking that Haden, our father's backstabbing friend, wanted it."

"We found out later that everyone in power on Merwin wanted it," Nickel said. "The King of Merwin and the other leaders in the Zukar. Now they can't ever get it because the treasure is split in four pieces."

"Pieces?" Jade asked. "Did you hide it after we left Merwin?"

Daniel cleared his throat, not knowing exactly how he wanted to tell her the truth. "No, the pieces are spread between you, Nickel, Faulk and me. The pieces are now *within* us. And we can only ever use it when we all are of the same mind, the same goal, and are together."

Jade sat up and away from Daniel. "You mean to tell me I have part of a treasure inside my body? And if we ever want to use its power again, I have to be with you? And Nickel, uh, and Faulk? Is that why you want to…"

Daniel leaned in and kissed her. She softened, and he deepened the kiss. Dragging his lips from hers, he held her chin in his hands. "I want to be with you because I'm in love with you. I made a big mistake before you lost your memory that may cost me you…and your love forever, but I'm working, will work, every day of my life to show you that I'm sorry. And to be with you, not to use some stupid treasure, but just…to…be loved by you."

171

A tear slid from the corner of her eye. "I believe you, and I think I'm falling a little bit in love with you. But I don't know…" She pushed him away, turned from him and buried her face in her hands. "Everything's so confusing, and this sucks, I just want my family back the way I remember them, but the memories are in bits and pieces. I don't…don't even know if what I feel for you now is real or when I get my memory back if I'll even remember this time with you."

Daniel wrapped his arms around her, pulled her slight form between his legs and held her close. "Just take a moment at a time, and when we get Gabe and Michael, things will work out."

Jade took several slow breaths, and wiped her eyes clean of tears. "Okay, then, maybe we ought to just get to it. I'm rested now and want to beat up something."

"Good, then, Nickel, let's go," Daniel gave Nickel's shoulder a push.

"About time." Nickel grinned and crawled onward.

They traveled a few moments and Nickel hesitated. A portion of it was opening and closing, and voices filter up throughout, vibrating the surface under their knees.

Daniel put a finger up to his lips and crawled in front of Nickel. Estimating the distance he knew he could use his body as a bridge for theirs. Daniel stopped next to Jade and whispered in her ear, "I'll lay diagonally. You and Nickel climb across. You go first."

Jade nodded and whispered in Nickel's ear.

Daniel slowly pushed himself forward, bracing himself over the opening. He bit back a curse at what he saw below. Hunt fiends, mid-sized, muscle-packed flesh eaters. The guards were feeding them. Their bodies were similar to earthly bulldogs, but they had no hair, only slick lines that had small holes in them called sniffers.

One of the guards spoke as it tossed some flesh into the huddle of four hunt fiends, "The warden believes the new slaves have gone free, but he can't track them on the system."

Daniel's body tensed as he felt the tentative push of Jade's hand on his thigh. Sweat beaded on his forehead, and he gritted his teeth as he strained with every fiber of his flesh to remain completely still.

Jade slipped.

Daniel froze.

One of hunt fiends growled.

The guard tossed it more food.

Daniel hissed out an errant breath, and relief flooded him as Jade recovered and finished climbing to the other side.

He stilled again as Nickel started his crawl, and his light form skittered across Daniel quickly as though he understood the strength it took for Daniel to hold the position. Digging deep, Daniel gripped the edge of the opening, pushed his legs up and balanced before doing a back flip to quietly land on the other side.

Jade mouthed, "Wow" and started to crawl. Daniel returned a nod and Nickel sped forward.

Daniel seethed. Part of him wanted to beat Michael to a pulp for taking things this far. But he couldn't blame Michael totally; it was his idea to come to this…hellhole. They would make it out and save the sorry souls who were trapped here. Breaking into Uukin to save the kids and women, he knew were pawns in the King of Merwin's determination to rid Merwin of the families who owned riches no one in the universe could believe, proved he was stupid. The more he thought about it, the more it seemed that the King of Merwin wasn't working this angle alone. Daniel would bet his sorry butt that the ruler of the Zukar nation had a bent on this, and if that was the case, then he'd wanted Michael to deliver what? The answer was easy: the famed treasure the Warden held close—the one thing in the universe known to allow its user to control the minds of men, not just one man at a time but to bend the will of millions.

Jade gasped. He turned in time to see her sliding forward with Nickel frantically holding onto one of her legs.

Careless. He'd been careless. He grabbed Jade's leg and pushed Nickel back out of the way as she struggled to remain calm. Daniel saw it in her face, then he looked down and held back the bile that bubbled up in his throat.

There were no screams, only the stricken look of frozen fear on the faces of the women who were bound, gagged and being dropped one by one into a large metal machine. That was bad, but Daniel held firm while Jade dragged her eyes from the gruesome sight spouting out from the end of the grinding machine. Cans. Tons of them that said FOOD.

30

Daniel stopped in front of the final opening in the venting system. Beads of sweat formed on his brow as the guards shuffled the group of slaves and inmates forward deep into the dark mine. Below him, the crudely chiseled walls of the tunnel emitted a faint gas and the men who cut away at the rock bodies were drenched in sweat on their bare backs. Children were scattered between the men, their eyes a strange hue of glowing whites.

"The guards—won't they see us?" Jade inched closer to Daniel to lean over his shoulder.

"No, we'll blend in with the others. They only have two guards posted near the one exit." Daniel adjusted himself and took another search around to make sure there are no additional guards or dangers around them.

"What's wrong with those kids?" Jade asked.

"They send them in to dig out eggs. It's one of the major supplies the warden sells to other lands. Those eggs are from the Manawats, a beast of energy that only lives here. Children are used to steal its eggs since the things don't find children threatening. Once they reach a certain height, the things will attack if you touch their young, and electrocute anything around them."

"Oh, but their eyes."

"They go blind after a while. It's a side effect of touching the eggs. The reason they have to enslave more children each year. Sad to say, the Zukar is a major supplier, thanks to the King of Merwin capturing and imprisoning orphaned kids here." Daniel tapped Nickel on the head. "It's time."

"I'm ready." Nickel tucked his slingshot in his pocket and grabbed onto Daniel's arm.

Daniel lowered him to a protruding rock, and Nickel waited for the huge guard to turn around before dropping to the ground between two small children who appeared to be waiting patiently while the larger men were digging.

"Your turn." He timed it right, and dropped Jade to the same ledge that Nickel had used. One of the slave men spied him, put a finger to his mouth and signaled to Daniel to wait. Daniel nodded back, noticing the Zukar tattoo on the man's neck, and smiled in relief.

"Send in more of the children!" the guard called.

It took every bit of Daniel's concentration to hold still as one of the guards lined up the children who ranged from six years or so, to twelve. The men, Merwin-born and humanoid Zukar, moved and cleared a path for the children. Nickel was shuffled with the younger kids and Jade was hidden behind some of the Zukar prisoners.

Daniel balled his fist, angry that he couldn't do anything to stop this, to protect Nickel, and to destroy the bastard guard who would harm these defenseless kids. He knew what happened to the females after a certain age, and the males if blind and helpless were probably put to death and turned to food for the others. This was why he knew down deep the King of Merwin and the Zukar ruler were working together to send children and unsympathetic Zukars, who were either washed up thieves or those who fought the system, to Uukin. They must have a deal with the Warden. Merwin was powered by the scattering of these precious eggs. They could be strewn throughout any world to provide an almost magical source of power that didn't need to be physically built, only tapped into. But Daniel knew in his gut that there was something else, he'd have to figure how Michael fit in all this.

Daniel let go a breath when the guard turned back to the exit door and allowed the kids to dig for the glowing eggs with their bare hands. Nickel stayed toward the end of the line, seemingly waiting for a spot closer to the dugout portion of the mine. The air was thick, heavy and almost stifling as Daniel held back a retch.

One of the men pushed another into action and he fell against the guard. Several others followed and Daniel dropped to the ground, thankful for the diversion. But just realized there was only one way out of there to the Warden's quarters: through the guards.

Daniel elbowed one of the men beside him. "I'm here to help everyone rise up against the Warden. My father was Rayne from the EBRA sect of the Zukars."

The older, work roughened man frowned at him, "I knew him. He was the best, but you…" He nodded at Daniel. "You're just a kid. How are you going to pull this off?"

"Your help. Do you know how to get to the Warden's wing? I want to shut this place down – free everyone." A commotion ahead made Daniel look up. Jade was pressed close to the wall, hidden behind one of the younger men, and Nickel was crouched close to the ground beside her.

"I'd only been forced to go there once, and it was a violent episode I'd prefer to forget. But that's the only way to the control system that will shut this place down. You can only get out through that door there." He pointed.

"Then what, where do I go after that?" Daniel slid out one of his knives from his boot and handed it to the guy.

"After we create a diversion for you, head down the hall, don't stop no matter what, 'cause you gotta catch them by surprise. Dispose of the guards, leading to the hall where they keep the women and children. I have a daughter there, and they've been trying to dig their way out for over a year." He grunted. "But if you can kill the guards standing there and get past them, just open the gates along the way. The girls will do the rest."

Daniel started to stand, but the man's hand stayed him. "One more thing. The locking systems are near the Warden's living quarters just outside the guarded area. Whatever you do, deactivate the locks first. It'll set everyone free – and we will be able to help you destroy the Warden. That mean, sick bastard's got it coming to him." The man spat.

"It's as good as done. Let's do this." Daniel stood in time with the Zukar prisoner.

The man let out a war cry and the place broke out in chaos. Daniel stood firm, pushing down the anxious energy that threatened his control. He dragged Nickel up, sliding his way through the middle of the fighting crowd.

"This way!" Daniel pulled out his gun from his waist, "fight it out!"

The guards were chopping away at men and children as if they were rag dolls. Daniel fought the anger that threatened to spill over at their sacrifice, all due to his stupidity. Just as the guard was going to slice down a young boy, Jade threw her knife with perfect precision, cutting through the guard's wrist.

Another man grabbed Jade's knife and stabbed upward into the guard's neck. "Run! It's clear!" the man screamed and everyone stomped and trampled over the fallen guards. But others came, and the men fought behind Daniel as he ran, dragging Nickel behind him.

Daniel dipped, swung Nickel around and jabbed his knife upward while Nickel pounded on a huge beast's head. Jade threw darts one after another with stronger and stronger force, never missing her mark of the guard's eyes, blinding them as Daniel shot them down.

Then they ran.

"Keep throwing them!" Daniel demanded and worked on the lock blocking the corridor closed.

"There's too many! The men are dying." Jade's hand went to her hip. "I'm out of darts!"

"Damn." Daniel kicked at the lock once more, then Nickel slid under him and pulled out a pin from his pants.

Nickel worked the lock then hit it. "Got it."

"Good Nick! C'mon." Daniel slammed his shoulder against the door. It opened, pushing Nickel until he fell over. Daniel caught him by the collar and pushed him forward. Jade kicked the door closed and ran behind them, keeping time.

Daniel heard it first. The rumbling at the doors behind them, just as his eyes landed on the lower vent. "Quick! There."

Nickel slid in front of the vent, opened it and crawled inside. Jade followed him and Daniel pulled up the rear and closed the vent.

"Go! Go! Go!" Daniel pushed Jade's back as they crawled. Commotion and fighting filled the hallway behind the vent.

Daniel's heart beat rapidly in his chest, and his eyes jumped around, looking for the any sign that they were nearing the Warden's quarters. The sound of water rushing below them echoed, and the screech of urchin up ahead stilled him a bit. But he couldn't stop, he had to find Michael and Faulk before they did something stupid, before Michael betrayed everyone who loved him, and before Faulk got hurt.

He'd never be able to regain Jade's love if her brother killed his cousin. And there was no way Daniel would hurt Michael – even though he really wanted to.

He glanced at Jade and wondered at why she frowned. And he realized that lately his own mistakes kept hurting her—them. How he'd ever make it up to her, he didn't know. His heart, he guessed, would always be with the Zukar, even if he continued to fight against it.

Daniel felt it. That energy flushing through his blood. The thing that called him to this life. The life of a thief, the one he'd been groomed for.

The tapping of little beasts vibrated the ground in front of them. The sound of sloshing water got stronger.

"Are we almost there?" Nickel asked.

"Just about, but I don't think we'll be able to stay in here until we run into it," Daniel lifted a hand to stop Jade from squeezing past him. "There's something up there."

The sound grew and seemed to multiply, and the swish of water seemed to pound the metal around them.

"We have to go through it. If we don't, there'll be more guards," Jade surmised. "And I'm out of darts." She hit her belt several times. "The belt's not producing them anymore. It must be jammed."

"Here." Nickel handed her a knife he pulled from his boot. "It's my extra."

The sound tapping of clawed feet got louder, and within minutes hundreds of beasties resembling rats with no hair and red eyes came at them.

Daniel kicked at the vent opening above them. "Ugh! Help me out here." He twisted back the metal piece that held it in place, and glanced at Jade who was working feverishly at the other.

"They're coming too fast!" Nickel shoved at the vent just as one of the beasties jumped on his back. "Aaah!"

"Let them come with us!" Daniel pushed open the grate and helped Nickel up as a few of the beasties started climbing on him, nibbling at his clothes, biting the flesh on his hands.

Jade hopped out of the vent, swatting some of them out of her hair. Daniel followed and the beasts charged out behind him in waves, blanketing the floor. Guards shot at them in the commotion, there was banging on some of the doors in the dark hallway that led to another corridor ahead.

"Set them free!" Daniel ran and slid to one of the doors, pushed the button on the side and it swung opened. Women and children poured into the hall.

"I got this one," Jade hollered and pressed the latch on the door nearest her while kicking some of the beasties off of her and ducking the slashing whip of a guard.

Daniel rushed a little girl out of the way. His eyes landed on the guard in front of him just as the blinding slap of the electric whip wrapped around his neck.

31

Faulk slowly followed Michael's lead. He gathered a wad of spit in his mouth and chucked it out between his teeth into the thick, dark, and stinky waters. His hand slipped down to his waist and inside where the hidden pocket holding the flat, gold egg he'd lifted from Michael.

Stupid. Stupid. Stupid. He'd meant it as a joke, but part of him held onto the thing because Michael seemed to have an unnatural possessive streak when it came to the piece, and Faulk wondered at it.

"How much further?" Faulk asked, hoping this time, Michael would acknowledge his request. But Michael didn't turn his head or spare him a glance.

He heard squeaking, but refused to yield to his fear of what was within the waters. Faulk wouldn't give Michael the ammunition to taunt him about his uselessness. Faulk may not have been born a Zukar, but he had four years of flight school training and was at the top of his class in strategy training and defense. But even those accomplishments seemed weak compared to Daniel and the others.

"This way," Michael grunted and pointed down another tunnel that seemed to have less water.

Part of Faulk wanted to hate Michael, but he couldn't. Michael was Jade's brother and at one time, Faulk thought he was in love with Jade. But Daniel beat him to that, and now Jade was one of his best friends. After what he, Jade and Daniel had been through to retrieve the treasure Daniel's father hid, there was no way he could hurt Jade by hurting her brother. Even if the creep was trying to get them all killed.

They fought against the current of sludge to turn down the tunnel with less of the putrid liquid.

"Are you sure you want to do this? I'm not stupid. What you are proposing will get Gabe and Jade killed. Don't you care about them? " Faulk stepped up behind Michael to avoid one of the green glowing fish that was climbing the sludge-splattered wall.

Michael stopped cold, kicked a glowing fish out of his way. "They will survive. You need to worry about you and yours. Me and mine will be getting out of here with what I came here for."

"You selfish bastard!" Faulk's fist lifted.

Another flat fish, with hooked claws, climbed up the wall, squeaked. Within minutes, others followed them up the wall.

Faulk hesitated. "Dude, it looks like something's…" One of the fish jumped off the wall and onto him. Its flat side opened and teeth clamped down on Faulk's leg. "Argh!"

Michael ground out a whisper, "Shut up before the rest of them attack! They can't see but sure has hell can hear you."

Another fish followed.

Faulk deflected a few of the fish that jumped at him. He tried to keep it up in silence, but a grunt or curse escaped and more of the fish attached to him. "I need a knife," he demanded of Michael. A fish bit at his hand, and he slapped it against the wall, then pried its teeth from his hand. Another launched at him and he ducked, just missing a bite to the head.

Michael slapped down a few and stabbed some in flight. "Never. Give me what I want, tell me where the damn egg is, and I'll save you," he spat back. More fish attached. He sliced a few.

"When we are all safe, I will tell you where it is," Faulk responded with barely a whisper. His eyes suspiciously watching the remaining fish attached to the dirty walls, breathing rapidly as if they thirsted for their next attack.

Faulk caught a shadow of Michael's smile.

"Now you're talking sense." Michael pulled out his gun. Fired a shot at the wall near Faulk, then laughed as the surrounding fish launched towards Faulk.

Faulk screamed.

32

Daniel fought against the jerking of the whip around his neck. It didn't help. He'd have to go with them. The grumbling guard tugged at it and the whip slid down his neck, wrapped around his shoulders, his arms, and hips, stunning him to numbness where it touched. Through the fray of commotion, the guards were being pushed and attacked by the maelstrom of prisoners. The open area was shaped like a hexagon with dozens of doors. The doors were all open. Everything was in chaos as the slaves fought off guard attacks. Escaping slaves fought off guards while trying to unlock the other doors on the opposite walls. Several of the doors burst open with the flooding of more prisoners who piled into the fray.

Daniel searched frantically for Nickel and Jade, but couldn't find them anywhere. Daniel took several slow breaths and prayed they were safe. He had to get to the Warden's quarters. That was where Michael would be heading and it was the only way to get control over the prison.

But he didn't want to go on without the others. So he pulled back against the restraints. The guard's layered face of skin spun around at him, and growled.

"Let me go! I'm nothing to you." Daniel tried to distract the guard by screaming.

A large prisoner came from behind him and hit the guard on the head with a club.

"Argh!" the guard roared.

Daniel kicked forward into its stomach and landed another kick to its face. The male prisoner hit the guard several times from behind. The guard's heavy body hit the ground and the slave twisted the club upward, then stabbed down into the guard's meaty face, crushing it into fleshy pieces.

"Get out of here. Cut off the security mechanisms before they blow this place up!" the prisoner told Daniel before rushing off to attack another guard.

Daniel picked up the whip from the guard. His eyes traveled through the mayhem and spotted a guard seeming to rush out through a hidden exit. Taking a quick survey around for Jade and Nickel, his chest pumped at realizing he'd have to leave them.

"Damn!" He ran after the guard and slid into the doorway just before it closed on him. The hidden exit was dark, with the exception of the glowing whip the other guard had in its hand. Daniel was behind him, making his steps light and keeping some distance. The guard didn't seem to notice him.

"Warden! Warden! It's imperative you let me in." The guard banged at the door at the end of the hall. Its alien accent riddled with pops and clicks between words.

Daniel waited. He rubbed anxiously at the handle of the weapon before moving forward with each loud knock the guard made on the other door. The guard didn't see him coming, didn't immediately feel Daniel's knife poised at its neck.

The door opened.

Daniel hit the guard on the soft side of his neck with the butt of the whip. Then pushed through the open door before the Warden had time to close it.

The Warden stood there, tall, alike in looks to the guard but with similar characteristics of a Merwin. Instead of the wrinkled, almost-burnt looking skin of the guard, the Warden's skin was smooth over its eyes, nose and cheekbones. But wrinkled and burnt tight skin covered his neck and clawed hands.

"You are?" the Warden asked in a deep but clear human tone.

Daniel stepped forward and pointed his knife at the soft base of the Warden's neck. "Here to get the treasure you hide in this place."

The Warden smiled at him. "Really? And who sent you? Dante, the weak King of Merwin?" The Warden sniffed. "You reek of the place." He waved a hand and slid back.

Daniel stepped forward, the knife steady. "Why would he want this from you? Tell me, and help me and my friends get out of here."

The Warden lifted an eyebrow. "Out of here? No one's getting out. I'll incinerate the entire planet first. The agreement I have with your weak king and the Galactic council is that I run this planet the way I want, in order to keep the universe safe from the most dangerous creatures known in history."

"What about the Sira Zukar—the king of the Zukars that live on Merwin? He would come get us." Daniel knew it wasn't true, but he wanted answers and figured the Warden would bite for a while.

The Warden laughed. "Really? He's been feeding me his weakest baggage and slaves for decades so he can pillage the riches of those gone. He'll never come and save you. The bastard's too greedy. The King of Merwin, the Sira Zukar and I have adhered to the treaty of our forefathers for almost a century. They would never breach these walls for a rumored treasure. And if they did," the thick twisted skin above his eye lifted, "I have ways to bring them under control."

Daniel pressed the knife more firmly against the Warden's neck. "The treasure you hold, I want it. Take me to it."

"Never. I'll kill you first. I'd burn this place to the ground and release the level 5 creatures into the universe. Is getting something that belongs to me so important? I thought you wanted to save your friends? Yourself?" The Warden stepped closer to the knife, it dug in and a dribble of green blood seeped out of the small wound. "You see, I'm not the one in trouble here. You are."

"Not true. Your prisoners are freed and trust me, they're mad as hell at you for the beatings and the side effects of mining energy for you to sell to keep this operation going And if they knew that you fed them their own flesh and blood children and weak ones, you would've had a revolt long before now." Bile rose in Daniel's stomach at the atrocities he'd seen.

"I knew there were some setbacks, but that will get under control when I incinerate those wards." He took his finger and slid it through some of his blood before popping the finger in his mouth. "And I will get more – from Merwin, of course."

"You'll never have enough to keep mining those eggs of energy." Daniel's brow started to sweat and his arm was heavy, but he didn't move it. If the Warden incinerated those areas, Jade and Nickel would die. Gabe wouldn't make it. And he'd have no one left.

The Warden's warped lip lifted. "I have other ways to make money. And to make the odds work in my favor."

"How? Your treasure? The one that gives you the power to control the minds of others? That's already gone." Daniel bluffed.

"Then there's nothing left to save you from." He dropped to the floor and pulled out a small gun. Shots of scattered silver specks spit forth from it.

Daniel dove for the chair but fell after being hit with several of the pellets. The banging on the door on the far side of the room got louder. Within seconds, it burst open with hoards of prisoners, being led by a limping Gabe.

Jade ran to Daniel's side. "Daniel! Daniel! Oh no." She pressed her hand against his bleeding shoulder.

Dizzy for a moment, Daniel moved his head from side to side. "I'm okay," he answered hoarsely. He struggled to push himself up. Daniel forced down the bile in his throat and was pushed back with Jade on his sore arm as a large prisoner attacked the Warden.

The Warden's gun fired rapidly, but the burly prisoner kept charging.

Daniel surged forward. "Noooooo!" The prisoner's knife sliced clear through the Warden's neck.

Gurgling through the spurting blood, the Warden spit out one last word, "All will die," and slapped his hand on the button on his chest.

"We gotta get out of here." Gabe pulled Daniel and Jade up with Nickel on his heels. "Now!"

Daniel shook his head and staggered away from Gabe. "We can't. The bastard Warden just set off the bomb to incinerate the place. And if the level 5's aren't secured, no one is safe. There's only one thing we can do."

Gabe ducked and turned as he followed a limping Daniel through the chaos. "Are you crazy! C'mon!" He grabbed Daniel's arm.

"Get everyone out of this ward while I search for this damned treasure your brother wants."

Daniel jerked his arm out of Gabe's grip. His wounds, thankfully flesh wounds only, would have to hurt until he was done. The only thought in his mind was how he would stop this disaster he'd started. He had to get them out. Where was Franz when he needed him!

33

Michael heard hammering and pounding about them. He checked on Faulk who limped behind him. Almost there. Almost done. He was close to finishing this. If it wasn't for the fact that some part of him wanted to get off this planet and back home to Merwin to see his parents, make sure they were safe, he'd have killed Faulk a while ago.

Being a Zukar had taught him the waste of showing mercy. The Zukar King hadn't given any to him or his brother. Michael bit back the taunting memory of Franz's screams. And he was ashamed of the tears he'd shed from watching his brother's pain, from begging to give anything to make them stop. It wasn't the way he'd been trained by his father or Haden, their former leader of the EBRA sect of Zukar that were a specialized group of thieves who took on the most difficult jobs. Sure, they'd taught him how to do the deed, but dealing with true torture, guilt and all that went with it, had come with the hard lesson of experience.

He pounded on the circular door above them. Faulk didn't make a sound. Michael figured the lesson he'd taught him earlier kept the nuisance quiet. That was best, he didn't need Faulk making him second guess why he'd come to this stank place. Why and who was most important was his own flesh and blood. Michael would save his parents. His weak brother Gabe could never do it. Neither would Franz. Since Michael couldn't bring himself to confide in Franz of all the tortures they'd both endured at the hands of the Sira Zukar, Franz couldn't see the sacrifices Michael was making for him – for all of them.

"Are you ready to tell me where my egg is? If I don't get it, I have no excuse to keep you alive. None at all." Michael spat back at Faulk.

Faulk cleared a tortured breath. Cuts and blood littered his face and damp neck. "You'll get it as soon as I lay eyes on Daniel. I'll tell you where I hid it, *on him.*"

Michael raised an eyebrow at the last few words Faulk uttered, something about the way he said it made Michael wonder if Faulk was holding something back. He wanted to punch the idiot for causing all this trouble, but there was no time for it. His fingers worked quickly at unscrewing the small metal pieces that held the door in place. Then without looking back at Faulk, he pushed the door open and shimmied up the ladder.

"C'm here decoy." Michael held out a hand to help Faulk up. The commotion outside the room was a muted succession of yells and pounding.

"Thanks, I think." Faulk hesitantly took Michael's hand, the distrust evident in the frown on his face.

"Something I've gotta do first." Michael wiped his hand down his damp shirt and yanked out a small pointed tool. "It's in here, the treasure." He tugged Faulk by the hair over to the metal wall design on the right wall of the small chamber.

Faulk struggled. "You promised I'd see Daniel first!"

"I lied, like you did. You have it, I know it, heard the hesitation in your voice when you tried to throw me off by saying Daniel had the egg on him." Michael tore at Faulk's shirt, his vest, then waist.

Faulk punched him and fought back as hard as he could. Michael countered and punched him back, loving it. Smiling at it. Faulk stumbled backward. Michael kicked him in the chest, charging Faulk as he fell. Michael landed punch after punch to Faulk's bloody face, holding Faulk in place with his knee to Faulk's squirming chest.

Michael's eyes landed on the egg that fell out of a slit at Faulk's waist. "I knew it...you..." He raised his knife, staring into Faulk's shocked expression.

Daniel burst through the door. "Don't do it!" then he charged at Michael, knocking him onto the floor.

Daniel jumped onto Michael, wrestling to snatch the knife out of his hand. Michael jabbed at him, and Daniel ducked, elbowing Michael in the chin.

"Get off me!" Michael yelled and head-butted Daniel in the nose.

"Give me the knife! Stop this!" Daniel punched Michael.

Michael twisted out of Daniel's reach and stabbed downward, slicing through Daniel's shirt. More thundering feet stormed the area. Screams and jeers from the guards continued. Explosions and fire sounded off on the floors above them. Michael jabbed Daniel in the side and pushed him off of him.

Daniel struggled up, ran after Michael and tackled him just after Michael slapped the flat gold egg into the crusted symbol of a spider on the metal wall.

The floor began to shake. Daniel's fist tightened against the frustration bubbling up inside of him. "Michael, you'll kill everything?! For what?!"

Gabe screamed, "Michael! Stop! The Level 5's will be set free!"

Michael ignored them and reached inside the small door on the wall that opened. A clear bottle shaped like a teardrop held a glowing blue liquid within it. A jewel framed the top of a small opening with jagged sharp metal pieces.

Michael pivoted around, his eyes boring into Daniel's. "I'm saving my family. From you and your stupid father. It was the only reason I agreed to leave Merwin to come to this rotting planet with you. To get to this treasure and to deliver your head in return so the Sira Zukar would allow my parents to live."

Gabe charged him. "You bastard!"

Daniel stood still, fighting for calm as he digested every word. The structure around them was in chaos. But nothing mattered, only that Michael had accused him of putting his parents' lives in danger, of putting Jade and her entire family in danger – because of their love for him and Nickel. He stepped forward and wrestled Gabe from Michael, whose eyes had never left Daniel.

"This is bigger than you –than me, Michael. The Level 5's will be unleashed into the universe if we don't secure this prison. Then all of us will die, we'll be hunted by the Galactic Council and your parents will be dead since the closest planet to Uukin is Merwin."

Michael's left eyelid twitched. Daniel held a struggling Gabe close to his chest by bracing his arms around Gabe's shoulders and crossing his fingers behind Gabe's neck.

Gabe kicked out at Michael. "Dad wouldn't have allowed you to do this, Michael. I'm your brother. Franz and I would've helped you save them."

Daniel nodded. "I would've given my life to save your father, Bry. He's like a second father to me – and you and Gabe, like my brothers. I'm sorry, so sorry I caused this. Let me do right by them. Let's repair this."

Micheal sank to the floor, he slowly lifted up the treasure. "You're right, my father would never forgive me for this. For wanting to kill you, for carelessly leaving Gabe behind to do this, for…everything." His hand went through his hair. "I'll fix this. I'll become the new Warden of Uukin and keep the Level 5's imprisoned."

Daniel released Gabe.

"You don't have to do this alone." Gabe limped forward. "We'll stay and help you."

Michael stood, thrust the treasure into Gabe's hand, and pushed him out of the way. "No, you and Daniel, go save our parents, destroy the Sira Zukar, and I'll take care of Uukin." Michael ran to the Warden's chair.

Daniel rushed forward. "Stop! It'll change you!"

Michael kicked Daniel out of the way and sat down. "It's too late. I changed the moment the Sira Zukar tortured Franz in front of me." The large metal chair spewed spikes. They pierced Michael's skin. "Argggggggh!" The whites of his eyes started to glow green, he growled and grew. The skin on his face burned, stretched and pulled until he resembled the guards.

Michael surged forward, his voice several octaves deeper than before, "GET OUT! NOW!"

34

"**R**un!" Daniel practically dragged Nickel along. Pushing through the crowd of fighting prisoners and guards, he was determined to get them out of there alive. Now with Michael as the new Warden of Uukin, Daniel didn't know how much time they'd have before the prison was secured again. Even now, he heard the clicking that signaled locks were being replaced and floors were being reinforced.

A girl fell in front of them, grabbing onto Faulk's arm. "Take me with you! Please! Please!"

Faulk grabbed her up and helped her to walk. "We got another one!"

Daniel grunted. He barely had time to save them, couldn't bring others with them, but he hoped Michael would do the right thing and free the prisoners who were too young or not guilty. Daniel wondered if the change of the chemicals pumped into Michael's skin changed his mind, twisted it to become as evil as the previous Warden.

"There! C'mon," Daniel ran toward the elevator shaft. The doors were broken and open but the elevator was several floors below them.

Gabe handed him the treasure. "You take it, I know you'll be better able to keep it safe."

Daniel looked down, his chest tightening at the responsibility Gabe just handed over to him. "I got it, I'll finish this for Michael." He slid his knife from his hip. "Grab the cable, I hope it's powerful enough to get us all up. I'll take Nickel and Jade with me." He nodded towards Faulk. "You take care of my cousin and his baggage."

"Got it." Gabe slapped him on the back.

Jade stepped up and wrapped her arms around his neck, and Nickel grabbed him around the waist.

"Hold on!" Daniel secured his hand around the first cable then cut it. Straining with the excess weight, his other hand grabbed the cable higher and he looped it around them as they shot upward several levels. Bouncing a few times in front of a closed elevator door, he and Jade landed several kicks and the door jarred open.

He swung the cable and they jumped on the platform just as Gabe and the others arrived. "We're almost there. Hurry," Daniel commanded and Jade straightened.

"Do you smell smoke?" Jade pointed ahead. The hallway was filled with a light smoke.

"That means the place is cleansing. Michael can't be doing that?" Gabe asked as he grimaced to stand.

"The Warden will do it. Soon the place, the planet will be on fire," the girl with Faulk said. Her sticky blonde hair was plastered to the side of her face.

"But there's a new Warden. He wouldn't set the place on fire." Daniel stepped closer to the girl, inspecting her, and realized that she was Merwin born, with gills on the sides of her neck.

"It doesn't matter. Whoever becomes the Warden is controlled by the creatures within the planet. They are no longer of free mind." She blinked her large blue-green eyes.

Jade exhaled. "What did we leave Michael to? Oh no." She covered her mouth with her hand.

"We have to go! The place is going to blow up!" The girl trembled. Then wrapped her arms around Faulk.

"I say we follow the directions of the native," Faulk answered. He pushed past Daniel.

"Yeah, cuz, I think you're right." Daniel grasped Jade's hand. He glanced at Nickel who was close behind him and pointed down the hall. "That's the way outside."

"Guard ahead!" Gabe called.

Daniel released Jade's hand and charged the guard blocking the exit. The guard swiped his sword that glowed on the end with the bluish blood of a Merwin prisoner, then snapped his electrically charged whip at Daniel. Daniel bobbed and weaved. He dropped to the floor. His foot jabbed out and kicked the ankle of the guard. Jade threw a knife at the guard's face, piercing his one and only eye that sat in the middle of his thickly skinned face.

"Let's go!" Daniel almost hesitated at the sight ahead. Fire was everywhere. Prisoners fighting guards, the ground rumbling. rocks sliding and only a few trucks around. "To the truck. Over there." He pushed Nickel. "Don't stop running till we get there."

He ran as fast as he could, kicking and punching at the guards that lunged at them. Finally, he made it to the large block framed truck without doors, and fumbled around the rudimentary dashboard.

"Let me pick the lock." Gabe reached over the back seat and slipped a sharp tool from behind his ear.

Daniel heard pounding feet behind them. "Hurry! They're coming!" He gulped and hoped the truck would hold together to get them to their ship. He flashed a hand over the communicator embedded in his inner ear. "Franz, we're coming your way in a burning truck, meet us halfway."

"You're kidding, right?" Faulk gawked.

"Nope." Daniel flicked a switch near the steering wheel and the doors slid out of the sides, closing them in, and the windows slid up on the sides. "Hold on!"

Daniel pushed his foot on the accelerator—heart racing—and blazed a path right into the trees of fire.

"Oh no, he's going to kill us!" the girl cried.

"Daniel, are you sure about this? This truck's not gonna last." Faulk pounded Daniel's seat with his fist. "Go back!"

"I won't. We-can-make-it." Daniel hoped, his hand tightening on the gear shift. He pushed the pedal to the floor and twisted and turned out of the way of falling trees, splintering wood and tumbling rocks.

"The heat! It's burning up in here. Daniel, go faster!" Jade fell against him.

"I promise, we'll get out of here." He flashed a hand over his ear. "Franz! Where the hell are you?"

"Not far, about two more miles and you'll outrun the fire. I'll lower the ladder for you to get into the ship. But make it quick."

Gabe leaned in between Jade and Daniel. "Hey, can't you tap into the power from the pakeet and heal this world? Maybe that would help save Michael from its darkness and make it livable for the slaves here?"

Beads of sweat poured down Daniel's face. "Not now, we have to be of the same mind, mental center, and Jade…doesn't remember anything that includes me, and when she does, she'll hate me even more."

Faulk chimed in, "We don't have a choice but to try. We're gonna be burned alive!"

Fire licked the inside of the truck, melting the windows and the frame.

"Not today!" Daniel plowed through the thick simmering brush and into a clearing free of trees.

Daniel skidded to a stop, and pushed the smoking door open. "C'mon now! It's gonna blow." He pulled Nickel over the seat. Making sure Jade and the others got out, he ran, pulling Nickel further away from the truck. Within seconds, the vehicle exploded.

"The fire's still coming. Where's Franz?" Gabe limped around, looking upward.

"I don't know, he's not answering." Daniel sighed, this wasn't looking good. The fire was building up and would be upon them in minutes. He had no choice but to do what Gabe suggested. "Nickel, Faulk we have to do it. We have to call to the pakeet to heal this planet. It's the only way."

Nickel stood up. "But Jade? Can she do it if she doesn't remember it or what happened?" Nickel grasped Jade's hand.

Daniel turned to Jade, leaned over and kissed her lips. She hesitated but a moment before kissing him back. "Jade, I'm sorry I didn't tell you this earlier, but here it is. I love you. When your mother first placed you in my arms and told me I would be your protector. But I don't deserve your love. It was a mistake coming to this godforsaken planet. We've lost everything here. Ourselves, your brother and because of my stupidity, Merwin, our home. But we have something to fight back with. Aliens gifted us with a treasure, one that can heal worlds, but it only works when we are in extreme danger…and when we all agree to use it – together."

She frowned. "We? As in I have this thing? Can it really be inside me? How do I use it? I'll help any way I can…because I love you too, no matter what happened to us before."

With a wry smile, Daniel replied, "I only hope you still will. Grab my hand, and just focus on healing this place."

Jade's hand tightened in his. Faulk grabbed Nickel's, and within seconds, a stream of red, blue and gold lights snaked out from the center of their chests to meet between them. Winds whipped around them and the ground shook beneath them. The tornado of light between them shot into the air. Thunderclouds gathered and multiplied in size in an instant, sending blankets of rain down on them.

"What's happening?" The girl beside Gabe grabbed him at the waist.

"They're changing this place, bringing it back to life." Gabe steadied her and watched the tornado of beautiful lights pour out of the others like waves.

The air grew sweeter, the trees blossomed, grass grew at their feet and the ground trembling settled. The rain stopped, the clouds receded, and a sprinkling of fire-ravaged grass poked out of the blackened dirt. The process seemed to take forever, as if time slowed. They all stood watching the world blossom.

Daniel recovered from his trance just as Jade collapsed. He caught her in his arms, and caressed her face. "Jade? You okay? Please say you're okay."

She blinked, focusing. "Daniel…oh, Daniel, I'm sorry." Jade kissed him, hugged him tight. "I remember everything, everything. God, I was so stupid to think you were being selfish by protecting me all the time. You…you did it because you loved me." She kissed him on the lips once more, as she savored it, hungered for him. "Like I've always loved you."

Daniel's communicator went off and Franz's baritone voice came through loud and clear, "Hey? What the hell just happened? This place is like freakin' paradise! Did we fall into some type of time warp or something? I'm right here."

Jade stood up, and Faulk and the others came closer. She smiled at Daniel. "I sure am not telling him what happened."

Faulk laughed. "Me either."

Gabe slapped Daniel on the back. "Not me."

Daniel smirked. "Aww hell. I will since I've been set up." He pulled Jade to him and landed a smacking kiss on her lips. "But trust me, I will repay the Sira Zukar for what they did to you and your family. I owe Michael that much. Merwin, here we come."

And he felt it, that old feeling—the one he got every time he set out for his next job, his next adventure, the next challenge where he tested himself, and hoped, he'd survive.

BOOKS BY
LM PRESTON

PURGATORY REIGN SERIES

Peter Saints' life stinks. But things are about to get much worse. First, his parents are murdered in front of him. Then another victim dies in his arms. Visions plague Peter with warnings that something wants him for a sinister cause. It desires the one thing that Peter refuses to give, his blood. Peter carries within him the one gift or curse that could unlock a secret to destroy the human race. On the run with Angel, a scruffy kid, Peter starts to unravel the mystery. It is the one treasure the heavens sought to hide from the world. Unfortunately, when Peter finds the answer he hopes that will save the girl he loves, he opens the door to a great evil that happens to be salivating to meet him. Purgatory Reign is Book 1 in the series including Deviant Storm, Fierce Tides and Colliding Souls.

Purgatory Reign, Book 1
Deviant Storm, Book 2
Fierce Tides, Book 3
Colliding Souls

THE PACK SERIES

Teen, blind, vigilante on a mission to save the missing kids on mars. Shamira is considered an outcast by most, but little do they know that she is on a mission. Kids on Mars are disappearing, but Shamira decides to use the criminals' most unlikely weapons against them, the very kids who they have captured. In order to succeed, she is forced to trust another, something she is afraid to do. However, Valens, her connection to the underworld of her enemy, proves to be a useful ally. Time is slipping, and so is her control on the power that resides within her. But in order to save her brother's life, she is willing to risk it all. THE PACK-RETRIBUTION, Book Two in THE PACK series.

The Pack, Book 1
Retribution, Book 2

THE BANDITS SERIES

Bandits, Book 1
Wastelands, Book 2

LUV SERIES

Dawn, the neighborhood tomboy, is happy to be her best friend's shadow. Acceptance comes from playing football after school with the guys on the block while hiding safely behind her glasses, braces, and boyish ways. But Tony moves in, becomes the star Running Back on her school's football team, and changes her world and her view of herself forever. Other books in the Summer LUV series include: THUNDERING LUV and DOUBLE TROUBLE LUV

Flutter of Luv
Thundering Luv
Double Trouble Luv

MIDDLE GRADE

Explorer X – Alpha
Explorer X - Beta

ACKNOWLEDGEMENTS

There are many times in my life when I'm inspired. God gives me the thirst to write but places amazing people in my path to nudge me. This story was inspired by my writing group, the Columbia Writers. They encouraged me to come out of my box and write a short story in first person. Then my daughter, my ever-vigilant supporter, read it and suggested that I craft it into romantic episodes between the two characters. I thank them for these wonderful nudges they gave me.

More Releases From Lm Preston

www.lmpreston.com and blog: http://lmpreston.blogspot.com

ABOUT
LM PRESTON

LM. Preston was born and raised in Washington, DC. An avid reader, she loved to create poetry and short-stories as a young girl. With a thirst for knowledge, she attended college at Bowie State University, and worked in the IT field as a Techie and Educator for over sixteen years. She started writing science fiction under the encouragement of her husband, who was a Sci-Fi buff, and her four kids. Her first published novel, Explorer X – Alpha, was the beginning of her obsessive desire to write and create stories of young people who overcome unbelievable odds. She loves to write while on the porch, watching her kids play, or when she is traveling, which is another passion that encouraged her writing.

You can find out what Lm Preston's up to on her blog:
http://lmpreston.blogspot.com and new releases
http://bookpartylmpreston.blogspot.com

www.ingramcontent.com/pod-product-compliance
Lightning Source LLC
Chambersburg PA
CBHW020324260626
47156CB00004B/1365